T0106438

Remembering
Lucy

IAN STUART

Order this book online at www.trafford.com
or email orders@trafford.com

Most Trafford titles are also available at major online book retailers.

Printed in the United States of America.

ISBN: 978-1-4907-1310-6 (sc)
ISBN: 978-1-4907-1309-0 (hc)
ISBN: 978-1-4907-1311-3 (e)

Library of Congress Control Number: 2013915339

Trafford rev. 09/12/2013

 www.trafford.com

North America & international
toll-free: 1 888 232 4444 (USA & Canada)
fax: 812 355 4082

Introduction

What an amazing girl she was. Harry could not believe his luck when he met her. It was love at first sight. She was 22 years old and just finishing her Bachelor's Degree in Tianjin, China and he was 59 living and working in Beijing. They met by chance at an Education Exhibition which was being held in the China World Conference Centre. He almost lost her in the crowd but they found each other again and their romance began. She had everything as far as Harry was concerned, not only was she very beautiful and incredibly intelligent with good social skills, but she was also caring and loyal with a great sense of humour. What followed was her continued education, travel to different countries, love, fun and happiness until the time came when the bottom dropped out of his world.

Beijing

As far as Harry knew, 26 Feb 2005 was not a significant date in history, but it was a very special day for him—it was the day he first met Lucy. The chance of him meeting her was millions to one. He was living and working in Beijing with a population of over sixteen million, and she was living some sixty miles away in the city of Tianjin, with a population of over twelve million. Their meeting really was millions to one, and it must have been destined by the gods.

How had the gods managed to arrange that the these two should meet at an education exhibition that was being held in the China World conference centre in Beijing, next door to the China World Hotel? It was nothing short of miraculous that they should both be there at the same time, so their meeting each other must have been pre-ordained. He was taking part in the exhibition, trying to promote a new idea for his education and immigration business by assisting Chinese students to identify which career path would be most suitable for them. Lucy was there representing a Chinese education agent from Tianjin.

He saw her briefly as she walked—or as he always said, floated like an angel—by the stand he was working on, and he was immediately attracted to her. As soon as he could get away from a crowd of students who were asking him lots of questions about the computer programme he was promoting, he walked in the general direction she had taken, praying for a miracle that he would be able to find her. There were thousands of people at the exhibition, which occupied two floors of the exhibition centre. Five hundred different universities and colleges from thirty-five countries all around the world had purchased stands to try to encourage the thousands of Chinese students visiting the exhibition to undertake secondary and tertiary studies at their particular educational establishment. Harry was going to have to be very lucky to be able to find her in such a heaving mass of humanity.

Thankfully his prayers were answered, and he eventually spotted her standing in one of the corridors which ran alongside the exhibition hall, handing out flyers to potential clients as they walked into the exhibition. She looked absolutely stunning in her light brown business suit, and she seemed very confident in what she was doing. Her skin was slightly darker than most Chinese; it was a light honey colour, more like a Filipino or Thai. She looked so beautiful, and her hair, which was naturally black and straight like most Chinese, was dyed a dark brown colour; she had had it permed so it cascaded down her neck in gentle waves. She had high cheekbones, and her sparkling eyes, which were very mischievous, were almond shaped and were quite wide apart.

He was truly smitten. He decided that the only thing he could do was to go and stand near her and hand out some flyers for his own company. After a few encouraging smiles, he managed to overcome his natural shyness and introduce himself. Her English was very good, and they spent quite a long time talking in between handing out flyers, before she had to go back to the stand which her agent had commandeered; he had not actually paid for the stand, like all the other exhibitors, but had taken over one which was not being used. Lucy spoke English with an American accent, because all of her English language teachers at her university, Tianjin University, were from America. She told him that she was in the last couple of months of her four-year bachelor's degree in English and international business. Before they parted company, he managed to persuade her to give him her e-mail address so that they could keep in touch with each other, and he gave her one of his business cards, which had his name, e-mail address, and mobile phone number on it.

Harry was looking forward to seeing Lucy on the second and final day of the exhibition so that he could invite her to have lunch, but she was nowhere to be found. He neglected promoting his business ideas for a couple of hours and searched both floors of the exhibition centre two or three times over, but he could not find her anywhere. He couldn't even find the stand which the agent she had been helping had been using. She had completely vaporised into thin air just like the morning mist.

That evening, once the exhibition was over, he sent her an e-mail, hoping upon hope that she had given her a real one. He asked how she was and told her how nice it was to have met her. He mentioned that he had been hoping to see her on the final day of the exhibition, in order to invite her out for lunch.

To his absolute delight, he received an e-mail from her the following morning saying how nice it was to have met him. She explained that she was sorry that she was not able to see him on the second day, but the agent she had been helping had decided to return to Tianjin after the first day of the exhibition instead of staying for the second day. She also told him that she was busy preparing for her final examinations.

Once their initial contact had been established, they exchanged polite e-mails every few days, and he was beginning to suspect that he had found a pen friend, or at least someone who just wanted to practice her English writing skills, and that was all it was going to be.

Much to his surprise and absolute joy, she sent him an e-mail three weeks after their first meeting saying that she was coming up to Beijing that weekend with an aunt, and asked whether he would like to meet up. He was thrilled at the prospect of seeing her again and immediately sent her an e-mail saying that he would love to meet her again. He gave her the name and address of a German bar and restaurant, Schindler's Anlegestelle (or in English, Filling Station), and he suggested a time they should meet.

The owner of the restaurant, which was situated at the edge of Ritan Park along Guang Hua Lu, not far from the British embassy, had a very interesting history. He had been the military attaché at the East German embassy in Beijing until the two Germanys combined, when he found himself out of a job. He therefore returned to Germany briefly to do a butchers course—an unusual decision for a former senior military officer, but one which proved very lucrative for him. Upon returning to Beijing, he opened a butcher's shop, selling lots of really good meat and German-style sausages, which were made in his shop. He sold mostly to Western diplomats, Western businessmen, and the more affluent Chinese. He ran this business very successfully for a number of years before opening the German bar and restaurant, and his butcher's shop, which his wife continued to manage, sourced all of the meat for his restaurant. One of the restaurant's specialities, and the most expensive dish on the menu, was pork elbow, a massive piece of meat which was so big that lots of people who ordered them couldn't manage to eat them all. The only person ever known to have eaten it all at one sitting was an enormous German man who had been drinking litres of German beer before his meal—and then completely amazed everyone in the restaurant by drinking two or three more litres of beer afterwards. He must have had the stomach capacity of an elephant.

The German bar, as it was known locally, was a bit like a Nissen hut or an elongated igloo. It had a semi-circular shaped brick ceiling, and there were little alcoves along one side which had tables and benches in and were separated from each other by small walls topped with glass display cabinets containing toy German cars; diners could sit up to six at a table and have a virtual room of their own. Down the centre were lots of other tables where guests could sit, and along the other wall was the bar, where the drinks were poured. At the back of the restaurant were the kitchen and toilets.

Harry had reserved one of the little alcoves nearest the door for their first dinner together, because it was the most private of the alcoves and would allow them to talk quietly without having to raise their voices and be overheard by other guests sitting at the tables in the centre of the restaurant.

At the agreed time—well, slightly before—Harry was in the bar waiting for her to arrive trying to keep his excitement under control. He started to get a little anxious as the appointed time came and went, but after fifteen more minutes she phoned him saying that she was in a taxi at a petrol station about half a mile away. When she had asked the taxi driver to take her to the filling station on Guang Hua Lu, he had assumed that she wanted to go to the petrol station near the Japanese embassy. They laughed about it when she arrived, and it was a real ice breaker. They had a really enjoyable evening, and he began to realise what a very special and beautiful girl she was. She had an amazing vocabulary and was also extremely intelligent, with an excellent sense of humour—British humour, at that.

They talked non-stop all evening about lots of different things. She told him that she was living in a dormitory at the university with a group of other girls, even though the apartment where her parents lived was not very far away. Their apartment, which was in an old compound, was a little bit on the small side, with only a kitchen, a toilet and shower room, and a lounge. The bed where her parents slept was in the lounge, along with a settee, table, and television, so there was not very much room for her to stay now that she was a young lady. She slept on a camp bed on the small, enclosed veranda when she did go home, which was not very often.

She also told him that she did not get on very well with her father, mainly because of the way he had treated her mother over the years. He had had some very good jobs in the past in the fruit and vegetable industry, which involved him travelling to different parts of China to source fresh produce for various markets, and he had earned a lot of money but gave most of it to his girlfriends and very little to his wife. His wife and Lucy had to make do with what little he gave them and on what her mother could earn working as a kindergarten teacher and assistant. It had been a struggle for them both. On top of this, her father's family did not particularly like Lucy or her mother, and they made it abundantly clear to them that they were not part of 'their family'. It was a very sad situation, especially because Lucy's mother seemed to be a very kind lady.

During the course of their dinner, Harry told her how beautiful she was, and much to his surprise she told him that

Chinese people thought she was ugly because her skin was slightly darker than theirs. He could hardly believe that their vision of beauty was so different to his, but he thought himself lucky—their loss was going to be his gain. At the end of the evening, they walked back hand in hand to the small hotel where she and her aunt were staying. When they parted company, they had their first kiss, which Harry thought was really something else. Her lips were so full, soft, and tender. It was a wonderful, sensual kiss like he had never had before. He could have kissed her all night long and was reluctant to let her go. It was a case of one last kiss—over and over again. Eventually the cold Beijing winter weather got the better of them, and they managed to prise themselves apart before their lips got stuck together. They said their goodbyes with the promise of meeting up again as soon as her studies would allow. Their relationship was taking off and seemed to be moving to the next level.

He was walking on air as he returned to his apartment but had to decide whether he wanted their relationship to move as fast as it appeared to be doing. It was not a difficult decision for him to make—a no-brainer, as far as he was concerned. He wanted to be with her on a long-term basis. She was simply too perfect, and he could not let her go. She had everything—beauty, intelligence, good social skills, honesty, and kindness, as well as a great sense of humour.

There were a couple of minor problems, however. He was married in the UK and was already seeing another Chinese girl two or three times a week of whom he was quite fond. But after meeting Lucy, he realised that she was definitely the one for him and that he could not let his wife or his girlfriend stand in the way of developing a relationship with Lucy. The following Monday he informed his girlfriend that he had met someone else, and their relationship came to an end. Now there was the other minor problem for him to resolve—his wife.

After that first evening together, Lucy travelled up to Beijing every other Saturday so that they could meet up, have some lunch, and enjoy their time together before she caught the train back to Tianjin in the late afternoon. They spoke on the telephone almost every day and exchanged e-mails, with both of them looking forward to the next time she would be able to come up to Beijing, even if it was only for a short space of time.

It was during the course of lunch one Saturday that he told her that he was too old for her. He was thirty-seven years older than she was, and if their relationship became serious, he would probably be depriving her of her youth—she was only twenty-two. Twelve years younger than Harry's daughter. He explained that his feelings for her were getting stronger and stronger, so it was probably best for both of them if she found someone younger before they became too attached to each other.

To his amazement, she said that she did not want some young man using her body to work off his excess energy. She wanted more than that—love and affection, and someone who would take care of her and protect her for the rest of her life. The difference in their ages was not a big issue for her—she simply wanted them to be together. Harry was so pleased and somewhat relieved to hear this and it made him feel even more strongly about her. There was no doubt about it, he was falling madly in love with her.

The next time she came up to Beijing, he had to tell her that he was married. She was heartbroken and sobbed uncontrollably as they sat outside the Bleu Marine restaurant. She said that he was just trying again to get rid of her. This was the last thing on his mind—he simply wanted to be honest with her. He told her that his relationship with his wife was not a happy one, that he hardly ever saw her and had been thinking of getting a divorce from her for a number of years. However, because they basically lived apart, he had not found a strong enough reason for doing so—until he had met Lucy. Lucy was really sad and said that she did not want to be the catalyst that caused pain to someone she didn't even know, but he assured her that he wanted to be with only her and that she should not worry because he would sort everything out.

Just before Lucy graduated in June 2005, she told him that she was coming up to Beijing for the weekend. When he asked whether she was coming up with her aunt again and where she would be staying, she said that she was coming alone as usual and thought she would stay with him in his apartment. He was excited to have her come and stay with him. She already knew that he only had one bedroom, so he assumed—correctly, as it turned out—that they would be sleeping together.

He couldn't wait for Saturday to arrive. They met again in Harry's favourite restaurant, the Bleu Marine, which as the name suggested was a small French restaurant situated just off Chang An Avenue and almost directly across the road from the Silk Market. It is a very small restaurant with eight tables inside and eight tables outside on the patio, which ran alongside the pavement. It got quite busy at lunchtime and in the evening, but in the late afternoon it was generally quiet, a good place to stop off for a drink and watch the world go by. Their speciality was steak, and it was the best steak one could get in Beijing. The atmosphere in the restaurant was always very friendly, with Celine and her Danish husband Torben always made everyone feel very welcome. Harry used to go there quite often, and when he took Lucy along, the owners immediately befriended her as well.

Harry and Lucy had a leisurely lunch together before taking a taxi back to his apartment in the afternoon. She unpacked her little bag and took a shower. That was the first time he'd seen her naked, and it knocked his socks off—she was absolutely stunning from head to toe. She had small but very firm and beautifully shaped breasts, a beautifully flat stomach, and a very nice and round bottom. She was a goddess. After she had finished her shower and dried herself, he kissed her everywhere from her head to her toes. Her toes were also very beautiful and seemed to have a life of their own; she could move them all individually.

They eventually made love for the first time and it was her first time. She said that she had been saving herself for the right moment—unlike some of her classmates in her dormitory, who had already lost their virginity during casual relationships. It was a little bit painful for her at first, but he was very gentle with her, and they both knew that there would be lots of other times in the future when she would feel more comfortable.

They slept together that night and fell asleep in each other arms. Harry couldn't describe the feeling he had next morning when he awoke and saw her beautiful face sleeping peacefully on her pillow. She slept like a baby, with her arms slightly bent above her head. He woke her with a kiss, and she looked stunning even when she had just opened her eyes. After a few hugs and kisses he got up and made coffee and prepared a cooked breakfast for them whilst she was having a shower. The rest of the day was spent going out for lunch and drinks and shopping before she returned to Tianjin later in the afternoon, to prepare for her graduation ceremony.

They had talked about what she wanted to do once she graduated, and she had told him that she would like to live and work in Beijing in one of the nice new office towers, which had been built along Chang An Avenue, the main thoroughfare in the centre of Beijing. The following day Harry spoke to a British friend named Bill, whom he met every so often in the bar he frequented, to ask whether he knew of anyone who might be able to offer Lucy a job. Bill said that he had a Chinese-Australian girlfriend and knew for certain that she was looking for a personal assistant. Harry asked if he could speak to his girlfriend, Sarah, who was a director at an international real estate company with offices in one of the new office towers, to see if she was interest in interviewing Lucy. A meeting was subsequently arranged, and at the end of the interview Sarah offered Lucy the job. Lucy started work as Sarah's PA within a couple of weeks of graduating and moved in with Harry on a permanent basis.

Before she moved in, Harry did have certain reservations about her living with him full time, because he had heard stories from some other British men in Beijing who had allowed their Chinese girlfriends to move into their apartments—only to discover that they took over the whole place and insisted on watching only Chinese language channels on the TV all of the time, which most of the British men could not really understand. He therefore told Lucy a little white lie, to give himself a few days to think it over. He told her that his wife was coming out for a week and that he would not be able to see her during this time. He felt sure that she knew it was not true, but thankfully Lucy waited to hear his answer at the end of the week: a resounding yes. He wanted to be with Lucy all day and every day for the rest of his life. She had brought him so much happiness since they had met, and she made him feel like a young man again with his first real love—and she *was* his first real love; it had simply taken him a long time to find her. Harry had realised after meeting and being with Lucy that he had never loved his wife, in all the years that they had been married. What a wonderful feeling it was to be truly in love with such an amazing girl as Lucy. She had awoken feelings in him which he didn't know he had. His heart was absolutely bursting with love for her.

Lucy moved in with him after she graduated, and she started work almost immediately. Being Sarah's PA proved to be an excellent working experience for her because even though she had studied business as part of her degree and had listened to what her father used to tell her about his business when she was younger, she did not have the practical experience or the experience of office politics. At first she was a general go-for, running errands for Sarah, but it was not long before Sarah realised just how talented Lucy was and started giving her more responsibility and more interesting things to do, such as getting involved with the preparation of leases for companies who wished to lease property around Beijing. She also started meeting potential clients with Sarah on a regular basis and received a very good, all-around grounding in the retail leasing business, which proved to be extremely useful to her in later years.

Harry was still doing his education and immigration business and had moved to a new office space, which was within the same complex where he rented his apartment. It was a one-bedroom apartment, and he had converted it into an office. It was very similar but slightly smaller than the one he was living in, and was only about fifty metres away, very conveniently placed for popping home at lunchtime and as soon as he finished work in the afternoon. Before this he had been renting a larger two-bedroom apartment which had been converted into an office cum living space. It was okay, but as he got busier he had ended up converting the large bedroom into a studio apartment, and the rest of the apartment was office space. It was fine, but in order to go to the toilet, he had to walk through the main office, which meant that if he went to the toilet during the night, especially after an evening in the pub, he would often see faxes lying on the machine. As much as he tried to ignore them when he went back to bed, he found that he couldn't get back to sleep afterwards because he started thinking that they may be the replies for which he had been waiting. Inevitably he ended up getting up in the early hours of the morning and starting work. It was very tiring, and he never seemed to get away from work. This new arrangement was much better.

Lucy was working some long hours in the office. She left quite early in the morning to catch the bus and often did not arrive back to their apartment until a couple of hours after Harry had arrived home. He prepared dinner for both of them so that she could have some food as soon as she arrived home. Life with Lucy was wonderful. Sometimes they would meet for a drink in a pub or the Bleu Marine, which was quite close to her office, but most times she would go straight back to the apartment, where they would have dinner together. Harry used to watch her out of the apartment window each morning as she left for the office, and he'd watch her come home in the evenings. His heart swelled up each time he saw her walking home through the apartment complex's gardens.

At weekends they went shopping for groceries to Carrefours, a French supermarket chain that had recently opened a massive supermarket not far from their apartment. They also went to the world-famous Silk Market, which sold lots of imitation designer clothes and bags. The shirts, ties, watches, and DVDs were extremely reasonable, and even though they were not genuine, they were so cheap to buy that one could afford to throw them away within a matter of months if one decided you did not like them anymore. Some weekends they would take a taxi to various places of interest in Beijing, such as Fragrant Hills or Ho Hai Lakes. There was a very nice little bar and restaurant near Ho Hai Lakes called the Pass-by Bar. It was very quaint because it was situated in the middle of a large hutong, which was hundreds of small courtyard, single-storey houses, most of which were still occupied by extended families. This one had been converted into a bar with a little courtyard inside, where guests could sit to have a drink or some food. The food there was very good indeed, and Harry and Lucy went there quite often. They even walked there one Saturday morning—a two-hour walk from their apartment. Lucy was flagging towards the end and kept asking how much further it was.

They also found the time to go out for at least one meal each weekend as well. Sometimes to the Filling Station or the Bleu Marine, and other times to Chinese restaurants such as the famous Qingdao Beijing Duck Restaurant in the centre of Beijing. Mr Wang's Chinese Restaurant, which is within the diplomatic area of Beijing and not far from Lucy's office, was another favourite of theirs and was very popular because they served some outstanding food. Occasionally they would take the train down to Tianjin and stay in a nice hotel, usually the Crystal Hotel, so that they could meet up with Lucy's mother; sometimes her father came along.

A couple of months after she had started working for Sarah, Lucy came back to the apartment one evening and said that Sarah and some of the other girls in the office were planning a trip to Thailand for a week. She asked whether Harry minded if she went with them. He said that it would be nice for her to go now that she had a passport. She then asked him if he would pay for the trip. As much as he would have liked to have done so, he did not have enough spare cash at that time. She was very disappointed but said that she would work something out, because she really would like to go to another country so that she could get a stamp in her passport. She came home the following day and told him that everything was arranged. She had spoken to an old school friend, who had agreed to lend her the money, which she would pay back from her salary over a period of time.

The time for the trip came around a few weeks later, and Harry was very sad to see her go, but he wished her a safe journey and hoped that she would enjoy her holiday. He told her how much he loved her and that he would miss her whilst she was away; he would be counting the days until she came home again. As it turned out, he didn't think that she really enjoyed the trip. She was not a party animal or a big drinker, and on some of the photographs she showed him of the holiday, the rest of the girls were smiling while holding glasses of wine in the swimming pool and appearing to have a good time, but Lucy looked quite sad. Still, she had used her passport and had been out of China for the first time, which was her main reason for going.

They went down to Tianjin a few times after she came back to see her mother, and they even went down again for the Chinese New Year of 2006 to spend the celebrations with both her parents. The food her mother had prepared in her tiny kitchen was really nice. There were lots of dumplings, called jiaozis, and vegetable dishes. They ate in her parents' apartment. Around midnight, like millions of people all over China, they went outside into the communal garden area just outside of the apartment to set off lots of fireworks in order to scare off evil spirits before returning to the Crystal Hotel. Harry was of the opinion that her father, who was a few years younger than him, thought he must be old and decrepit, because he would not allow Harry to light any of the fire crackers in case he burnt himself. The noise of the fireworks was deafening. Millions of Chinese crackers exploded all over the compound and all over the city. Those small Chinese crackers really packed a punch, especially when there were hundreds of them linked together; when they exploded, they sounded like a machine gun going off.

On another visit to Tianjin, they stayed in their usual hotel and had lunch with her mother and father in a small local restaurant which was down a back street not far from their apartment. It was not very clean looking from the outside—a real greasy spoon sort of place—but the food was excellent. Whilst they sat at the table, with her mother and father opposite them, Lucy started stroking Harry's groin. It was quite exciting, but it was difficult for him to look at her parents, without looking like the cat who had stolen the cream. He felt sure that her father could tell from the expression on his face and the position of Lucy's arm that something was going on, but he did not say anything. That was the last time either Lucy or Harry saw him, and that was in early 2006. She really hated him and told Harry she was sure that if she had not been with Harry, her father would have already sold her to the highest bidder.

Shortly after their visit to Tianjin for the Chinese New Year of 2006, they started talking about returning to the UK so that Lucy could continue with her studies and earn a master's degree. She was very keen to do this so whilst Harry was on one of his very rare visits to the UK, to see his wife in East Yorkshire over the Easter period. He took the opportunity to drive his car over to Leeds to visit Leeds University. He had to make some enquiries on behalf of some of his student clients, and whilst he was there he spoke to a lady he knew in the Asia department to inquire about Lucy doing her master's degree with them. He had lived in Leeds when he was younger, and so he knew the area reasonably well. His sister and her husband, as well as some other relatives, also lived nearby—hence the reason for choosing Leeds. The lady Harry spoke to sounded very interested in Lucy's achievements and work experience so far, and she gave him all the necessary forms to take back for Lucy.

Within a short space of time of returning the application forms Lucy received a letter from the university offering her a place on their master's degree course in Chinese and Asia business, which would be starting in October. They immediately started preparing her student visa application. Lucy already had her bachelor's degree and had also passed the required International English Language Testing System (IELTS) with a good enough mark to enable her to study for her master's degree without having to take an English language course or a foundation course first. The rest of the documentation was pretty simple. Harry was going to be her sponsor, so he had to prove that he had the ability to pay for her tuition fees, accommodation, and food. Her visa was issued without any problems. Harry was happy for that, because he would have looked an absolute idiot if it had been refused—given that this was part of his job, to help Chinese students apply successfully for their student visas.

The next few months were quite hectic as they made plans for Lucy to go to Leeds. They needed to go shopping for some UK clothes and get her a laptop computer to take with her. They also had to book her flight and her student accommodations. Harry contacted one of his cousins, Gillian, who lived in a small village on the outskirts of Leeds close to the airport, to ask her if she would be kind enough to meet Lucy at the airport when she arrived and give her a bed for the night, until she could move into the university student accommodation the following day. Thankfully his cousin agreed to do this, and all their plans for Lucy leaving were in place.

The morning Lucy was scheduled to leave, her mother came up to Beijing to say her goodbyes and also to bring a few things which she thought Lucy might need in the UK. She insisted on trying to help Lucy pack her suitcases, much to Harry's amusement and frustration. Her mother's way of packing was to make bundles of clothes, wrap them up in a piece of cloth, and place them in the suitcase; they looked like large dumplings. Harry tried to suggest that clothes laid flat would be much easier and also would not take up as much room. Finally her mother accepted his suggestions, but worse was to come. She had brought a rice cooker up to Beijing for Lucy to take with her to the UK, to make sure she would get enough food. The woman was determined that it should go in the suitcase along with the rest of Lucy's belongings. It was turning into a farce, and they almost came to blows over that rice cooker. Harry kept saying that Lucy's suitcase would be overweight, and the rice cooker might get damaged in transit. He also told her mother that Lucy could easily buy a rice cooker in the UK. Her mother and Lucy were in tears at one stage when he kept insisting that they should not try to put the rice cooker in the suitcase. Her mother was adamant that Lucy should take the rice cooker with her because a Chinese-made rice cooker was much better than any she could buy overseas. Little did she know that a lot of rice cookers which are available in the UK are actually made in China. Eventually common-sense prevailed, and the rice cooker was excluded from the suitcase—although it did manage to sneak its way into Lucy's hand baggage.

That evening at the airport was a very sad moment for all of them, particularly for Harry and Lucy's mother. Lucy was sad to be leaving but at the same time very excited at the prospect of going overseas and studying for her master's degree in the UK. As she walked through to the departure area, after she had checked in, her Mother and Harry were gazing at Lucy and trying to imprint the last image of her into their memories before she gave them a final wave and disappeared from view. Even though her Mother and Harry could not communicate very well because his Chinese was very limited, he could tell that they both shared the same sad feelings. Neither of them slept very well that night because they worried about Lucy travelling to the UK on her own— the first time she had made a long, overnight flight. Harry felt sure that she would be okay, and he had every confidence in her ability to cope with changing flights in Amsterdam and negotiating all the immigration procedures when she arrived in the UK. Still, he could not help worrying about her until she called him the following day to say that she had arrived safe and sound, and that Gillian and her husband (neither of whom she had ever met before) had collected her from the airport in Leeds and had taken her to their house; they would be taking her out for dinner that evening. What a relief it was for Harry to know that she had arrived safely and was being taken care of. He couldn't thank Gillian and her husband enough for their kindness.

Leeds UK

The day after Lucy arrived in Leeds, Gillian drove her to the university, where she collected the keys to her accommodations in one of the student blocks about half a mile away from the university; the floor was reserved for post-graduate students. From what Lucy told him when she phoned after moving in, the room was nice but small. It had an en-suite bathroom with a shower, a desk for studying, a bed, and a wardrobe that was not really big enough for all of her clothes, but she said it was all right. It was not long, however, before she started telling him about some of the other girls who lived on that particular floor of the student accommodation and the noise which they created. One girl from Jordan, who had the room directly opposite Lucy's, seemed to have different boyfriends staying with her two or three nights per week, and a girl in the room next door, who was from somewhere in Africa, also had male guests stay with her from time to time. The walls between rooms were quite thin, so it was possible to hear what they were doing and saying. Harry was beginning to wonder what sort of place Lucy was living in—it sounded like a brothel. Luckily there were some girls from Thailand on the same floor who were

studying for their doctorates, and Lucy became good friends
with them. They used to cook meals together in the communal
kitchen.

A few weeks later, Harry took a flight back to the UK, to
see his wife and tell her that he was leaving her. He collected
his car and immediately drove over to Leeds to see Lucy. It was
wonderful to see her again, and he could not get enough of her
or stop looking at her—she looked more beautiful than ever. He
realised just how much he loved her and wanted to be with her all
the time and forever. He stayed with Lucy in her room, sleeping
on the floor because the single bed in the room was not really big
enough for the two of them; they had tried it, but it was not very
comfortable, and he doubted if either of them would have gotten
any sleep if they had both been in there together. They decided
that it would be best if Harry slept on the floor at the side of
the bed on a spare duvet. Lucy leaned out of the bed for their
goodnight kiss, and they went to sleep holding hands.

They spent a few days together and took a drive over to see
Harry's sister so that he could introduce Lucy to her and her
husband before driving up to the Yorkshire Dales to look at the
beautiful scenery. He also introduced her to fish and chips in a
restaurant in Skipton that he knew was good from previous visits
there with his parents when they were alive. She took to them
like ducks take to water and even made a chip butty with the
bread—she was becoming a real Yorkshire girl. On the way back
to Leeds, they stopped off in Otley, a beautiful little market town
which was not too far away from Leeds, and has a large Waitrose
supermarket where they bought bags full of food so that Lucy
could use it for preparing her meals in the communal kitchen.

Even though she had settled into student life in Leeds very
well, had opened a UK bank account, knew where to go to buy

various things, and was enjoying her studies, they decided, whilst Harry was there, that he should close down his business in China and return to Leeds so that they could be together. They both missed each other and loved each other so much that they didn't want to be apart. Harry contacted a friend at an English language school in Leeds who said that he knew of someone who wanted to rent out an apartment privately in the centre of Leeds—just where Lucy and Harry wanted to live. It was in a quiet area, within easy walking distance of the bus station so that Lucy could catch the bus each day to university, and was very close to the Royal Armoury Museum. It also overlooked the river and a sort of marina, called Clarence Dock, where canal boats and small leisure cruisers were moored—a perfect location. They arranged to rent the apartment starting at the middle of December 2006.

Harry returned to Beijing and started to close down his business. Once he had completed all the outstanding applications from his existing clients, he started to get himself organised for returning to the UK. He left Beijing in the middle of December as planned, and as soon as he arrived in Leeds, they moved into the apartment. Lucy was very happy to have him at home again, and she was also glad to move out of the student accommodation which had become almost unbearable because of all the nocturnal activity going on in her neighbours' rooms.

A few weeks before he left Beijing, however, Harry was invited out for dinner by an old Chinese friend whom he had known for a number of years. The venue was a very upmarket Chinese restaurant in the northern suburbs of Beijing that served the same kind of dishes which the emperor of China used to have served at his table hundreds of years ago. Upon arrival they were shown into a small, private dining room where they were met by a couple of young Chinese men who were joining them for dinner. Harry was introduced to them, and they told him that they owned their own company in Beijing which provided due diligence services on behalf of foreigners who wanted to invest in China, ensuring that any foreign company investing in Chinese companies would be investing in a viable business. It was a very nice evening because all of the Chinese people spoke good English so they were able to communicate with each other easily; the food was also excellent. At the end of the evening, they exchanged business cards and bid their farewells to each other, with the usual promises to do it again sometime.

About a week later, Harry received a phone call from one of the two young men whom he had met at the dinner. The man asked if Harry would like to go around to his office for a cup of coffee and to meet up again. Harry was not terribly busy at that time because he was already winding down his own business, so he agreed to go because it gave him something to do. Their office was not very far from his, so it did not take him too long to get there. It turned out to be in a residential apartment block quite close to the Carrefours supermarket. They seemed to have done what Harry had done to his office, in so much that they had converted an apartment into an office space. They had a cup of coffee, showed him around, and asked him what he planned to do once he returned to the UK. Harry explained his reasons for going—he wanted to be with his girlfriend whilst she was studying for her master's degree, and he would be looking for a job as soon as he arrived. After about forty-five minutes Harry took his leave, never really expecting to see either of them again before he left for the UK.

A few days later, however, and much to his surprise, they telephoned him to ask him if he would like to go out for dinner with them. Harry was on his own and did not have anything special to do, so he agreed. They met outside the restaurant the men had suggested on the west side of Beijing, and they took him in—again to a private room. This time, to his surprise, there was also a young Chinese man and a young Chinese lady. He was introduced to them, and as soon as the introductions had been made, the two young Chinese young men who had invited him to dinner announced that they had to leave because they had an urgent business meeting to attend elsewhere, but the young man and the young lady would take care of him. How strange.

His new dining companions spoke excellent English, and after they had ordered the food and drinks, they started asking Harry lots of questions about himself. They already knew that he had previously worked at the British Embassy in Beijing as Her Majesty's Consul (HMC) and head of the visa section before he resigned from the Foreign Service and started his own business in China. It wasn't long before they started asking him if he knew who was doing what kind of jobs in the British embassy at the present time. He told them that since he had left, some six years before, all the staff members who had been there when he was working there had reached the end of their tours and had been replaced by new people; he had no idea of who was doing what jobs now. He suggested that they get hold of a copy of the Diplomatic List for China, because that had all the details of the different embassies in China, and it also listed all the staff and indicated what their titles were and what jobs they were doing. They said that they had already seen this list, but they knew that some members of the British embassy had more than one job—some of them, besides doing the jobs listed in the Diplomatic List, were actually spies working on behalf of MI6, the British Secret Intelligence Service. Harry told them that he had no idea whether this was the case or not. They persisted for quite a while, saying that he must have some idea, but he maintained that because all of the staff were now different from what they had been when he was there, he could not tell them anything about any of the staff in the embassy.

The couple then tried a different tack and asked him what he planned to do when he arrived in the UK. He told them the same as he had told the other two young Chinese men—that he would be living in Leeds with his Chinese girlfriend and would be trying to find a job. They then asked him if he would like to help them when he arrived in the UK by joining the UK Falun Gong movement and attend Falun Gong meetings in London. They said that the Chinese authorities were becoming increasingly concerned that the Falun Gong movement was planning lots of demonstrations in China during the Olympic games, which was due to be held in Beijing in 2008, and that the Chinese authorities did not want this kind of thing to happen when the eyes of the world would be upon Beijing and China for the duration of the Olympics. He told them that Leeds was quite a long way from London, and he would not be able to go up there to attend meetings because he would be too busy working. They offered to pay his fares, but Harry said that he would not be able to spare the time. They were very disappointed that he could not—or would not—help them, and once the dinner was over they parted company. They told him that all of his answers to their questions had been very diplomatic—meaning that they had not gleaned any information from him.

Harry felt quite concerned about what had taken place and knew that he needed to report this approach to someone. He therefore contacted a man he knew at the British embassy who was a senior police officer from the special branch of New Scotland Yard in London. The man was in China trying to prevent the transportation of illegal Chinese to the UK by the so-called Dragon Heads, who used to ship hundreds of Chinese (mainly from Fujian province) to Europe and then try to smuggle them into the UK where they would look for work. Harry met him in the pub, where he usually saw him, and explained that he needed to speak to someone urgently but did not say exactly what it was all about. The police officer said that he would try to arrange a meeting.

A couple of days later Harry's friend called his mobile asking if he could go to the embassy straight away to meet someone. Harry was in the German bar at the time, so it only took him a couple of minutes to walk along to the embassy. Even then, Harry was still a little bit concerned because he knew, from the time he was working there, that one of the local senior Chinese security officers, who worked for the embassy, was there to watch who was going in and out and report it to the Chinese authorities. To his huge disappointment, this same man was in the security office at the gate entrance when he arrived, and he immediately recognised Harry. Harry was a little bit worried about him being there because he knew that his visit would be recorded and passed on to someone else, but he desperately needed to speak to someone about what had happened, so he brushed aside his concerns. He was quickly shown into the embassy and taken to the secure speech area, which he was familiar with from his days as HMC when attending ambassadorial meetings held in there.

The lady who came in introduced herself and said that she was the head of the MI6 cell in China. Before Harry could start talking, she said that she knew his previous history: that he had been Her Majesty's Consul and head of the visa section at the

British embassy in Beijing, and also that he had worked for MI6 some thirty odd years before that—they had long memories. She then asked him to tell her what had happened. It was such a relief to get it all off his chest and to feel that he had told someone in the right position about the approach that had been made. She made lots of notes and said that she was very grateful to him for reporting this to her. She also said that she was surprised that the people he had met did not know who she was, because she had been declared to the Chinese authorities as working for MI6. She went on to tell him that he should not worry, especially because he was due to leave Beijing in a couple of days; if he had any more problems before he left, he should contact her on her mobile number. Harry was not sure what happened after that, but he never heard any more about it and left Beijing a couple of days later. Leaving was a huge relief for him in some ways, especially after such a worrying experience.

Harry arrived back in the UK just before Christmas, and after he and Lucy moved into their new apartment, they did all the Christmas shopping for food and presents. They spent a very enjoyable Christmas together with no worries, and Harry didn't think about work. Lucy was doing well with her studies and amazed Harry by never making any notes on any of the lectures which she attended. She had a fantastic brain and could remember word for word what every lecture had been about; she wrote excellent assignments when required by her tutors. What a girl. She made Harry feel inadequate at times, when he thought about how many pages of notes he had made when he was doing his bachelor's degree.

Harry started making job applications in January once the festive season was over, but even though he was applying for three or four jobs every day, he was never called to attend an interview. He suspected that it was because of his age. Some of the jobs he was applying for were very basic, such as packing shelves in supermarkets, so it may well have been that he was overqualified as well as overage. After two or three months of trying without success, he decided that he needed to do something to keep his brain functioning and to occupy his time besides doing all the shopping, cooking, and cleaning. He therefore decided to take a distance learning course: Teacher of English to Speakers of Other Languages. It was an open-ended course with no set start date and no set finishing date—one simply worked at one's own pace. He tried to complete an assignment every couple of weeks so that he could post it off to the lady who was marking his work and who happened to live and work in Egypt. She was a British teacher specialising in English. It took him a couple of months to complete all of the nine assignments, but eventually he finished them all and received his teaching certificates, confirming that he was qualified to Teach English to Speakers of Other Languages.

Lucy was spending most of her days at the university, either attending various lectures or carrying out her own private research in the university library. She had her own favourite quiet little corner in the library where she used to sit and work on her studies. She told Harry that she was very happy to have him at home and also to be able to get on with her studies without having to worry about the domestic side of life. Harry was happy as well, to be able to take care of her and be with her every day. It was just about perfect—apart from him not having a job or an income.

He was still applying for jobs every day, but the longer it went on, the more futile it seemed; nobody seemed to want to acknowledge receipt of or even reply to any of his applications or letters. It was becoming very frustrating and a bit of a worry, because they were living on his savings. Harry was registered as unemployed and was receiving Job Seekers allowance, but because he had a pension from the Foreign Office, his weekly job seekers allowance was reduced to just over twenty pounds per week—even though he was not actually receiving his pension because it was being paid directly into his wife's bank account each month.

It was whilst he was searching on the Internet one day that he discovered that there was an immigration course that was being held in Manchester the following week. He thought that it would be an excellent course for him to do because even though he knew a lot about the requirements for anyone making a visa application overseas, he did not know very much about the requirements for people making applications in the UK. He enrolled in the two-week course and commuted to Manchester each morning. Lucy and he left the apartment each morning together, she for the university and he for the train station.

The course was very interesting, and he learned a lot about the requirements for applications made in the UK. It proved to be eight hundred pounds well spent because on the final day of the course, when he arrived back in Leeds in the late afternoon, he bought a copy of the local evening news paper, *The Evening Post*, and found an advertisement in the classified ads for a senior consultant for an immigration company which had offices in London and Sheffield. He phoned them immediately and was invited to go up to their head office in London to attend an interview the following Monday.

He met with the two directors, one of whom had been in the Foreign Office before transferring to the Home Office, where she eventually became one of the senior directors. She was in her late sixties or early seventies but was very active and knowledgeable about the requirements for all kinds of applications made within the UK. Their main focus at that time was applying for work permits for overseas nationals, which was something Harry was familiar with after having assisted clients overseas to apply for working visas once they had their work permits. The interview seemed to go well, and a couple of days later he received a phone call, followed by a letter, offering him a position as a senior consultant initially in the Sheffield office, but with the proviso that he would move to London to work in their London office as soon as Lucy had finished her master's degree. He was absolutely delighted, and so was Lucy when he told her. He started work at the beginning of July 2007 after seven months of unemployment. Everything was finally starting to take shape.

They had a comfortable lifestyle. Lucy worked hard on her studies, and Harry worked in Sheffield. That meant he left every morning quite early to catch the 6.45 bus so that he could arrive at the office in Sheffield by about 8.00. Leaving early and starting early, and not taking a lunch break, meant that he could leave work early in the afternoon to get home at a reasonable time so that he could have everything ready for when Lucy got home from university. They both seemed to be working hard at that time and did not have much time to go out during the week, but they did try to do something on the weekends, usually having a meal out somewhere on a Friday or Saturday evening. There was a little restaurant they particularly liked which was quite close to their apartment, called Restaurant 44 on the Calls, which was the name of a little cobbled street next to the river. They used to have an early bird menu, which ran from 6.00 to about 7.30 PM and included a free half bottle of wine per person, so with two of them having the early bird dinner, they received a full bottle each time they went—most of which was drunk by Harry. The food there was always good, the menu was quite varied, and they spent many enjoyable evenings in that restaurant whilst they discussed what they had done during the week and made their future plans.

There was also a fish and chips shop quite close to their apartment which had a 'buy one, get one free' special offer every Tuesday at tea time. Harry used to stop off there every Tuesday evening on the way home from work to buy fish and chips for them both, which they both enjoyed very much, and it also saved them cooking. Having said that, however, Lucy was a fantastic cook and could whip up a meal in no time at all. She used to amaze Harry by making two or three Chinese dishes when there was hardly any produce in the fridge apart from eggs, tomatoes, onions, and some broccoli. If it had been left to him, he would have probably made a Spanish omelette, but she used to prepare fried rice, egg and tomato, and a vegetable dish from virtually nothing.

London

Lucy finished her master's degree with a merit at the beginning of October 2007, and they immediately moved down to London. Harry hired a car so that they could put all of their belongings in it, and off they went. He expected that the drive would take them three or four hours down the M1 motorway, but he decided that because the part of London he needed to be in was on the east side, and the M1 motorway terminated on the north side, he would take the A1 road instead because that terminated close to where he wanted to be. The journey took them about seven or eight hours, and to this day he cannot remember where they went or what caused such a delay. They laughed about it afterwards, but it was a long drive—particularly for the UK. One could drive from London to Scotland in that time.

As soon as they arrived in the London area, he phoned his bosses, and they gave him the final directions on how to reach their office and the apartment where they would be staying. It had been agreed that they could stay in an apartment which was owned by the company rent free for the first three months, to give them chance to find a place of their own to rent.

The fully furnished apartment which they entered was amazing. It was in an old, converted warehouse in Wapping, alongside the river Thames. It had a large bedroom area just inside the door to the apartment, as well as a toilet and a bathroom. The rest of the apartment was one large kitchen and dining area that led into a lounge. At the end of the room were some large patio-style doors which opened up so that they could lean on the small balcony rail and enjoy the river directly below. It was fantastic and was a massive improvement on the apartment they had had in Leeds. The office where he would be working was in the same complex, on the ground floor, so he did not have very far to go to the office each morning and could pop home for lunch to see Lucy. It felt as though they were starting a normal life together.

They both loved London and living in the apartment. There was always something to see on the river, whether it was the large taxi-style boats ferrying commuters to their offices, pleasure cruisers, fast speed boats or warships paying a visit. The river was always busy, and they enjoyed watching all the movement. Most evenings they would stay at home, but they made a point of going to see a show (usually a musical) in the West End as often as they could, usually once a month. They generally had a meal in a restaurant and then went to the theatre afterwards. During their time in London, they must have seen about five or six shows altogether. It was a very lovely time, and they were so happy together. They used to walk along to Tower Bridge most weekends to do their shopping at the large Waitrose Supermarket, which was situated close to St Katherine's Dock. Sometimes they would do the shopping on-line and have it delivered—especially the heavier items which would have been too heavy to carry all the way back to the apartment from the supermarket. Lucy also loved going to the shops on Oxford Street and Regent Street, and they spent lots of time wandering around some of the large department stores, especially the designer clothes and shoes boutiques.

The only fly in the ointment, as far as they were concerned, was that Lucy could not find a job—even with two degrees and her fluency in English and Chinese. History was repeating itself, only this time for Lucy: she was applying for jobs every day and was only invited to attend one interview during the whole time she was applying. The interview was at a language school in one of the offices above the shops on Regent Street. Harry accompanied her to the interview, but when they got into the so-called school, it was a huge disappointment. It was one of the Mickey Mouse language schools which recruited students from overseas; supposedly to study English but who were in fact there to find work in low-paid jobs. Harry certainly did not want Lucy working there, and she did not want to work there, either. They returned home quite disappointed after stopping off for something to eat in the centre of town, and Lucy resumed her search for other jobs to occupy her time. It was not easy, particularly at a time when the economic depression was hitting lots of companies in the UK. People were being laid off all the time, and there were millions of people unemployed.

Lucy's graduation ceremony finally came around, so they both travelled up to Leeds for this special occasion. Harry had booked a hotel for them to stay which was quite close to where they used to live. He felt so proud as Lucy walked up on to the stage to receive her degree wearing her gown, and he wanted to stand up and shout something out, or at least start cheering, but when he looked at all the other parents, husband, wives, boyfriends, and girlfriends sitting quietly, he had to restrain myself and settle for clapping very loudly and long. There were some PhD students who were also receiving their doctorate degrees that day, and their gowns were a light Sherwood green colour and were much fancier than the MA students' gowns; they also had little Eliabethan style hats to wear. He said to Lucy afterwards that he would like to see her in one of those gowns one day with the little hat, adding that he was sure she would look very beautiful in that outfit.

They spent the night in Leeds and went out for a celebratory dinner afterwards to a nice restaurant, where he toasted her and told her how proud he was of her and how much he loved her, and that he would love her forever. The following day they returned to London, and it was back to work for Harry, with Lucy continuing her search to find a job—but to no avail. It was disappointing for her, especially being in London and with all of her qualifications.

One of Harry's first tasks when he got back into the office after Lucy's graduation ceremony was to prepare her international graduate scheme visa application form so that her visa could be extend by two years. This kind of visa was designed to give newly graduated students, be they bachelor's or master's degree or even PhD graduates, permission to stay on in the UK for up to two years after they had graduated so that they could gain some work experience before returning to their own countries. Lucy's existing student visa had only been valid for fifteen months and was due to expire in December, so it was imperative that her application for her international graduate scheme visa was submitted to the Home Office as soon as possible. It was submitted within a few days of them getting back, along with all the necessary supporting documents, the main one of which was her master's degree certificate as well as proof of Harry's continued support for her. He took her application down to the Home Office in Croydon personally and asked for it to be processed on the fast-track service, which meant that it would be ready for collection later that afternoon. They were both delighted and felt much happier once Harry had returned with her passport and new visa.

Lucy had remained in contact with her colleagues from the international real estate company in Beijing and had discovered that her ex-boss, Sarah, had already left the company and had moved to a local Chinese company which had started out by building tower blocks of small offices and home offices in various prime locations around the centre of Beijing. Sarah was now a director in this company. The company had moved on from its early beginnings and was now involved with building much more fashionable buildings for shopping malls and the like. It was in January or February 2008 that Sarah offered Lucy a job in her department, which was responsible for the refurbishment of a very famous historical street in the centre of Beijing, and for leasing out the retail premises along the street to lots of famous international brand companies. It was an opportunity that was too good to miss. Harry tendered his resignation, and they started to prepare to return to Beijing. It was good in a way, because the rent-free period on the apartment had come to an end in January, and he was now having to pay GBP1,500 rent each month even though his take-home salary was only GBP1,750. They were effectively having to subsidize their living costs from Harry's savings again.

Before they left the UK in May, in March Harry's divorce proceedings had finally reached the point where he had to attend the court hearing in Hull. He took the train up one day and stayed overnight in the Merchant Navy Club, which was adjacent to the railway station, and then he attended court the following morning. It was the first time he had seen his wife since he had left her two years earlier. She had been dragging her feet about the divorce, which was a pity because house prices had slumped considerably during this time, and their house was valued at a lot less than it had been two years earlier. She had also been busy trying to make lots of inquiries about what he had been doing whilst he was in Beijing, who he had been seeing, and where he lived and whether he was having any affairs. His wife had even phoned his former office manager to ask her if she was having an affair with him. She was also convinced that he had squirreled lots of money away whilst he had been there. Her barrister was of the same opinion, and no matter what Harry said, the man kept harping back to this. Harry told the judge quite honestly that he did not have any money secreted away in the banks in China and that whilst he was married to his wife, he had taken lots of money to the UK each time he went back and deposited it into their joint bank account. He also told him because of the changes in the visa procedures now in place, not only in Beijing but around the world, people were no longer required to attend an interview, and therefore his income each month had reduced drastically from when he had first started.

The judge was not entirely sure about this and seemed to be siding with his wife. He also asked Harry if he was presently co-habiting. Harry had been advised earlier that if he was asked such a question and denied it, then it could influence the judge's decision about who got what from the assets, so he admitted that he was. The judge then asked if he could ask how old she was—so Harry replied yes. After a pause where nothing was said by either of them, the judge said 'Well, how old is she?'

When Harry said twenty-five, his wife said in a loud voice, 'That is disgusting.' Not to Harry, it wasn't—it was absolute bliss.

They were called back later that afternoon to hear the judgement, which was not good news as far as Harry was concerned. The judge had decided that his wife should sell their large house and that she would receive two-thirds of the proceeds. Fortunately because their daughter, Joanne, was independent and living in Holland with her boyfriend, that she would not be included in any of the financial settlements of the divorce. The judge also directed that his wife would also receive the whole of Harry's pension from the Foreign Office. He was not very happy with this decision given that his wife had not worked for many years; she had sat at home all day long drinking two or three litres of wine and smoking two packets of cigarettes per day. He had been paying for everything, including her wine and cigarettes. But there was nothing he could do about it. However, after his wife had left the room in tears at the thought of having to sell their house, he said to the judge that it was the price of happiness, and it was. He was so pleased that his divorce had finally come through so that he could be with Lucy all of the time, and they could get on with their lives together without this hanging over their heads. They had already talked about getting married and had decided, even once he was divorced, that they would stay as they were—single, together, and happy.

Beijing

In May 2008, Harry and Lucy returned to Beijing and moved into a furnished apartment for a week in Century Towers, which was where Harry had lived previously in 2000 just after he had left the British embassy. It was about half a mile from their previous apartment and had been quite a nice apartment block when Harry had lived there before, but it seemed to have gone downhill a bit since then. They were not particularly worried because they knew that they would only be there for a short time until they found an apartment of their own to rent—and it was only a matter of days before they did.

They had called into a bar which Harry used to frequent, and he mentioned to the bar manageress, whom he had known for ten years, that they were looking for an apartment. She immediately telephoned someone called Chris, who was trying to find someone to rent his apartment so that he could move to the outskirts of Beijing, where he had a recording studio. She arranged that they could go around to his apartment the following day. It was ideally situated as far as they were concerned—about a five-minute walk from the office where Lucy would be working and where Harry hoped to be able to rent an office so that he could start up his business again.

The following day they went to look at the apartment, and Harry was surprised when Chris opened the door, because he knew him quite well—but he only knew his nickname, which was Elvis. He was a really nice American guy and showed them around the two-bedroom apartment, which was quite well furnished and in a nice, quiet block. They both felt that it was perfect, just what they were looking for—especially because it had a second bedroom, which Lucy's mother could use when she came up from Tianjin to visit them. They arranged to meet up with the landlord later that day, signed the lease, and moved in a couple of days later.

Lucy started work the following week and also helped Harry to get the necessary permission from the Chinese authorities to set up a company—in her name. She also managed to get him a small office space in the same office complex where she was working, albeit it in a different tower block. It was looking good for both of them. They would walk to the office together each morning and buy a cup of coffee on the way before parting with a kiss to go to their respective offices. Lucy enjoyed her new job and was busy every day, negotiating with both the Chinese authorities about what could and couldn't be done to the front of the new retail spaces in the street, which was being refurbished, and also relaying this to the various international companies who were interested in leasing retail space in this very desirable location. It was a difficult time for her because the Chinese authorities were adamant that only certain things would be allowed to be changed on their designs, and some of the international companies, particularly Apple, did not like the options presented to them. Negotiations were long and sometimes very difficult before both sides finally reached an agreement.

Whilst all this was going on, Harry had moved into an office space that Lucy had secured for him, and he was trying to kick start his business again—but it was proving more difficult than he had expected. He contacted his old office manager and told her that he was back. She immediately suggested that he contact one of their old agents who used to bring them clients years before. He did, and this lady came around to see him in the new office. She had provided him with quite a few good clients previously, and he was hoping that she would do the same again this time. Well, it didn't quite work out that way. She seemed to want to have a share in the business and also receive quite a large payment for each successful client she provided. Harry was not very happy with this arrangement but decided to give it a go and see how it went. She introduced him to a husband and wife team who came along and said that they could provide him with lots of clients, providing he could create supporting documents for them to submit with their applications. This was something Harry was not prepared to do—it went against the grain as far as he was concerned, to be manufacturing forged documents. However, they did start to send clients to him, and he did his best to prepare their visa applications as well as he possibly could. He soon discovered that most of the documents that they were providing were forgeries which they had created themselves. The visa section at the embassy were picking them up because they had much more sophisticated equipment now and were also able to phone various banks to check on whether a bank statement was correct or whether it had been doctored to show that there was more money in an account than there actually was. Most of the clients he had been given by this man and wife team were being refused because they were submitting fraudulent documents. That was not what he wanted, and it was not good for his reputation. He persevered, though, and was managing to survive by using his savings to subsidize the income, so that he could pay the rent and living costs. It was not an ideal situation.

Lucy's company had office parties every few weeks, to which Harry was invited, and he met lots of Kelly's colleagues—some of whom were very nice. They had a lot of fun at the parties, which were held on the ground floor of the office complex. He was so pleased that Lucy was happy and busy. She was learning an awful lot about negotiating with international clients as well as with the Chinese authorities.

Her mother came up and stayed with them for a few days from time to time, and it was always nice to see her. She did all the shopping and cooking whilst she was there, and she cleaned the apartment. Her dumplings were still fantastic, and they devoured them as fast as she could make them. Sometimes when Lucy was working late or meeting clients in the evening, her mother and Harry used to watch television together. One programme they particularly enjoyed watching was a Japanese programme called *Takeshi's Castle*, where lots of Japanese people participated in crazy games that resulted in them ending up in either water or mud, or falling off narrow bamboo bridges whilst having mini cannonballs fired at them. They laughed together, and even now, when Harry sees this programme, he still thinks of Lucy's mother and how much they used to love watching this programme even though neither of them could understand what was being said.

One evening, Lucy and Harry went out to a Japanese restaurant which he had been to before with an agent. It was not very far from their apartment, and the food there was excellent. They decided that rather than sit at a table and have waiter service, that they would sit around the eating area in front of where the chef prepared the food. It was a U-shaped area with the chefs working in the middle. They sat on one side of the bar and enjoyed the food, which was being cooked and served up piping hot.

It was not long after they had arrived that an older Chinese man and a young Chinese lady sat on the bottom part of the U-shaped bar and ordered their food. About twenty minutes after the couple arrived, Lucy said to Harry that the old Chinese man had said something very detrimental about her. When he asked what it was and when the man had said it, she told him that the old Chinese man had said to his girlfriend that the old foreigner (Harry) was having dinner with his Chinese prostitute. Harry was livid and asked when he had said this. She said it was almost as soon as they had sat down after they had arrived. It was too late for Harry to remonstrate with him after such a long time, and Harry's Chinese was not good enough to get his message across, but he made Lucy promise that if anyone ever said anything awful about her again, she should tell him immediately so that he could confront whoever said it. They might not be able to understand what he was saying, but they would get the message loud and clear from his tone of voice. It really upset him.

But what amazed him even more happened shortly afterwards. They had just ordered some more lemon chicken when this old Chinese man directed the chef to ask them if he could taste some of their chicken dish once it was prepared. Harry told Lucy to tell the chef that there was no way that they were prepared to let him taste their dish after what he had said about Lucy earlier. It was beyond belief how people could form an opinion about someone they had never met before and start pronouncing to the world what they thought.

The Beijing Olympics was not far away, and Harry's visa was about to expire, so he applied for it to be extended—only to find out that the Chinese authorities were not extending visas for any foreigners until after the Olympics were over. Hundreds of foreigners had to leave China during this time. In Harry's situation, it meant that he would have to leave China in July and would not be able to return until October, when he would be able to apply for his visa to be extended. It meant that he would be away for about three months before he would be allowed to return. Lucy was not very happy about this and decided that all they could do to prevent this from happening and ensure that Harry could stay in China was for them to get married, even though they had said all along that they wanted to stay as they were. Harry was not sure where he would have gone for three months or even what he would do if he had left. Marriage seemed to be the only option for them, and so Harry went to the British embassy consular section to post their wedding bands on the consular section notice board. They had to be posted for three weeks before he could receive written permission from the consular section that he was free to marry, and then he'd take this notice to the Chinese authorities.

Lucy's mother was also busy helping them in Tianjin, where they were going to have to get married because, according to Chinese legal requirements, Lucy had to get married in her home town. They got the necessary paperwork sorted out, and on 14 July 2008 they took the train down to Tianjin and met her mother, who took them along to the office where the ceremony would take place. She had organised everything and even paid for their wedding certificates. When they arrived at the rather bleak-looking office block, the place was almost deserted. They were shown into a large office, where they were asked various questions by a formidable, miserable-looking lady who gave them some forms to complete before sending them to another room where they had to sit side by side and have their photographs taken together. They were then ushered back into the other room and asked to sign a couple more forms before they received their marriage booklets, one for each of them. It was all over in a matter of ten minutes—as quick and simple as that. They immediately took a taxi back to the railway station, not even stopping for lunch, and caught the train back to Beijing. As soon as they got back, they started completing different visa application forms so that Harry could then apply for a visa as the spouse of a Chinese national. Lucy made him promise, now that they were married, that he would stay with her for at least fifty years. What a wonderful thought! Harry wanted to stay with her not just for fifty years but forever. Thankfully his new visa was issued pretty quickly, before his existing visa expired. It seemed a drastic step to take, but he loved Lucy so much that it seemed the right thing to do, even though he did not understand the reason for the Chinese authorities removing foreigners for the duration of the Olympics, some of whom, like him, had lived in China for years and had never created any problems. The Chinese minds worked in mysterious ways sometimes.

They knew that Lucy's work contract was only for one year and was due to end in May 2009, so they started to think about what they were going to do once her contract was completed. Harry had seen on the UK border agency website that the UK government was thinking about introducing a visa regime to Malaysia and South Africa, as well as some other countries, including Brazil. He had lived and worked in both Malaysia and South Africa before when he was working for the Foreign Office, and had fond memories of both countries. They decided that they would both travel to Malaysia first, because it was nearer, and then go to Borneo, where Harry had spent some very enjoyable times during his time as vice consul at the British High Commission in Kuala Lumpur. They got Lucy's visa and their flights organised, and off they went to carry out research on whether they really wanted to move there and what the work situation would be like if they did.

Borneo

They arrived in Kuching, the capital of Sarawak, on the island of Borneo and checked in at the Holiday Inn situated alongside the Sarawak River. This hotel was where Harry had always stayed when he went to Borneo on his consular visits from Kuala Lumpur. The hotel was still very nice and comfortable, but there seemed to be a lot more mosques in the area than there had been before, and they were awakened every morning at 5.00 AM with the calls to prayer (or as Lucy called it, 'sing a song time'). Harry couldn't remember it being so loud before when he had stayed there. They spent the first afternoon relaxing in the hotel and in the swimming pool. Lucy couldn't swim, so Harry was trying to help her to take her first strokes. It was a case of holding her stomach as she lay flat on the top of the water whilst trying to move her arms and legs, but it was not very successful. It was good fun for Harry, though, because she was wearing a biking, and he was holding her bare mid-rift in the water. They spent the next couple of days in Kuching looking around, and they even went out to the Longhouse, which Harry used to visit, stopping off at the Orang Utang rehabilitiation centre on the way there to see the Orang Utangs. They soon realised that Borneo was not for them, especially after living in Beijing with its sixteen million people; neither of them felt that they could live in such a small place, despite having found a really nice apartment in a beautiful complex just outside the CBD of Kuching. The job opportunities for Lucy were almost non-existent, and the amount of work Harry would be able to generate was also very limited. They returned to Beijing having decided to remove Borneo from their list—which left South Africa. As it turned out, a visa regime was not imposed on Malaysia, but it was on South Africa.

Harry had lived in Pretoria in South African during the 1980s and had really enjoyed his time there—the climate, the food, the people, and the rugby were great, and he was looking forward to going back there. He contacted an old friend and asked her if he could stay with her when he went over to carry out his research. She was pleased to have him stay, especially when he told her the reason for his visit. Her daughter was having a hard time finding something to do since she'd graduated from university and was interested in becoming involved with his visa business in South Africa. He booked a flight and went over on his own; Lucy could not spare the time from her work because the completion of her project in Beijing was drawing closer.

Upon arrival in Johannesburg, his friend collected him at the airport and took him to her house in Middleton, which was about half way between Pretoria and Centurion, north of Johannesburg. They made him very welcome and had a long discussion about what he planned to do and where her daughter fit in to the equation. Harry would need a work permit in order to work there, and they decided that they would set up a company with Harry, his friend, and her daughter all being equal partners in the business. His first port of call was to the head of visa section of the British High Commission, to introduce himself and also to find out how many visas they processed each month. The number was very encouraging. Whilst he was there, they also looked for office space situated near to the UK visa collection centre, where South Africans handed in their visa applications to apply for visas to travel to the UK. His friend said that she would arrange for someone local to prepare the new company website, and that she would get everything arranged for when he returned in May with Lucy. Things were looking good, and he left a few days later feeling confident that everything was arranged.

Beijing

When he arrived back in Beijing, it was such a pleasure to see Lucy again, even though she was pretty tired after working so hard towards the end of her contract. The refurbishment project was officially opened one evening shortly after he arrived back, and he was invited to attend the opening ceremony. The invitation to the opening ceremony was written on a Chinese silk fan, which had a picture of the street on it—how unusual but how Chinese. Come the evening of the official opening, Lucy and Harry were there early, but it wasn't long before lots of celebrities and television crews arrived to broadcast the opening ceremony. The street looked fantastic, and there were even some trams running up and down the centre, creating a world gone by. Harry didn't see so much of Lucy during the ceremony because she seemed to be busy with various clients, making sure that everything was all right with them. He did meet Sarah's British boyfriend, Bill, and they managed to procure a bottle of champagne, which they drank in one of the rooftop open areas above one of the designer shops to celebrate the end of the project. It was a fantastic evening, and Harry felt so proud of Lucy for being involved in such an amazing project that had transformed the old run down street into something really special.

There was a little bit of animosity building up, however. Harry knew that towards the end of the project, Sarah had resigned from the Chinese company and had started her own company, which had taken over the leasing of the retail premises. All of the staff who worked for her had also resigned and moved to her new company so that they could see the project through to its conclusion. As Harry understood it, Sarah had received millions of Chinese Yuan from the international companies as payment for what she had done for them—but she was reluctant to share it with anyone, including her staff. Naturally, neither her previous employers, who wanted a share of the cake, nor her staff were happy with this and started to put pressure on her to give them a share of what she had received. Sarah managed to avoid paying anything to the Chinese company but eventually succumbed to a lot of pressure from her staff to divide a certain amount of what she had received between them—still retaining most of it for herself of course. Lucy was disgusted when she was told how little she was going to receive compared to all her other colleagues—it was a pittance and an absolute disgrace. She was not happy, considering the amount of time and effort she had spent assisting Sarah, but she could do nothing about it. It left a nasty taste in her mouth, and she vowed that she would never help Sarah in the future with anything again.

They had already applied for Lucy's UK visa so that they would have somewhere to go if South Africa did not work out. They had applied for her to have what was called an indefinite leave to enter visa, which meant the same as having indefinite leave to remain in the UK. This kind of visa was good, in so much that one year after arriving in the UK, she would be eligible to apply for her British Nationality and a British passport. The rules for this kind of visa were that she had to be able to prove that she and Harry had been together for at least four years, which they had, and that they had lived overseas during this time, which they also had. Harry had asked someone at the Home Office in the UK about his interpretation of this when he was working in London, and he had been told that once Lucy and he had been together for four years, then they could apply for this kind of visa when they were in China. To make sure that this was going to be the case, Harry wrote to the entry clearance manager at the British embassy visa section in Beijing, asking her to confirm how she interpreted 'during this time'. Her answer was very vague and did not really explain what she was thinking. Writing to her proved to be a costly mistake because when they applied for Lucy's indefinite leave to enter, all they received back was a visa that allowed her limited leave to enter, because the entry clearance manager had said that they had not lived overseas continuously for four years but had been in the UK for eighteen months during this time. This kind of visa meant that Lucy would have to be in the UK for twenty-three months before she could apply for indefinite leave to remain, and then it would be another year before she could apply for her British passport. Harry and Lucy were upset about this, especially after he spoke to one of the entry clearance officers afterwards, who told him that if he had processed Lucy's application, he would have issued her with the indefinite leave to enter visa straight away, but because the entry clearance manager had been involved, she had insisted that Lucy only be given limited leave to enter instead. There was nothing they could do about it apart from grin and bear it.

As soon as they received Lucy's UK visa, they started to prepare her visa application for South Africa. Harry did not need one because he had a British passport and a letter from his friend in South Africa confirming that a work permit was being applied for, and that if there were any problems the friend would be responsible for the cost of his repatriation. But Lucy, being Chinese and travelling on a Chinese passport, did need an application. They completed her application form, and Harry took it along with her passport and other supporting documents, including their marriage certificate and his passport, to the visa section of the South African embassy in Beijing. The South African immigration officer who received the visa applications seemed very much full of his own self-importance and treated his customers with a certain amount of contempt. Harry handed over Lucy's application and was told that he would have to pay a RMB15,000 deposit to make sure that Lucy would return to China after her visit. Harry asked him to look at the documents and tried to explain to him that it wasn't a visit visa they were applying for, but the dependant of someone applying for a work permit. The man did not listen and instructed Harry to go to the bank to pay the deposit. Once he returned from the bank and handed over the application and proof of payment of the deposit, the visa officer accepted the application and told Harry that it would be ready by Friday, which was perfect because their flight was booked for Saturday.

They were all packed and ready to go and had given notice on their apartment to move out on Saturday morning. On Friday morning, Harry went to the South African embassy, as instructed, to collect Lucy's visa—only to be told by the visa officer that it was not ready but he could collect it on Monday morning at 9.00 AM. Harry asked politely if it would be possible to have it processed later that afternoon because their flights were booked for the following day, but the visa officer was adamant that they would have to wait until Monday. Harry was livid, and what made it even worse was that he could see, given the number of people who were applying for visas, that they were not terribly busy. How could the man do this to them? Besides, if it was going to be ready first thing on Monday morning, as soon as they opened, then it must have been processed by Friday afternoon. He left the visa section and tried to get in to embassy main entrance to speak to someone about this. No one was available, but he explained their situation to the South African person who was in charge of the reception area. She did not seem terribly interested, either. He left the embassy feeling really irritated and decided that he had best go to Singapore Airlines and change the flights to Monday, as well as book a hotel to stay in over the weekend. He was so angry with this visa officer that he decided to stop off in the pub on the way to the Singapore Airlines office to have a beer and calm himself down. It was lucky that he did, because halfway through his second beer, he received a phone call from the SA embassy visa section saying that Lucy's visa would be ready for collection later that afternoon. What a huge relief, and what a stroke of luck! If he had not stopped at the pub for a beer, he would have change their flights by the time he had received the phone call, which would have been quite expensive. Thank goodness everything was resolved. He collected Lucy's passport and made a point of going to thank the lady in charge of the reception area; he felt that she must have said something to the visa officer for him to have had a change of heart.

South Africa

They left for South Africa the following day, and Harry's South African friend met them on the Sunday at Johannesburg International Airport. She was pleased to see him and to meet Lucy for the first time. Harry and Lucy stayed with her and her son and daughter at their house for a couple of weeks until they found a house of their own to rent. Her house was on a large plot of land and was a big, old, single-storey property with three bedrooms and two bathrooms, a large lounge, and a games room, plus a kitchen. There were also three other small properties on the plot, which Harry's friend rented out to tenants. It was almost like a little township. Because everyone worked all day, Harry and Lucy were left pretty much on their own and spent a lot of time in the house and gardens playing with the family's two Rottweilers. They were practically housebound because they did not have a car. A car was essential in South Africa because there was very little public transport that went around the residential areas, so they were not able to go very far, apart from walking to the local shops that were nearby.

It was quite a difficult time for them especially because they realized that nothing had been done since Harry's previous visit. No website had been prepared, and no office space had been rented, so they had to start from scratch and do everything themselves.

They managed to find an office quite close to the place where South Africans submitted their UK visa applications, and they also found a partially furnished house to rent in a small, secure complex of six properties. There were three bungalows at the front of the complex alongside the road and three houses at the back, which faced a park and were separated from the bungalows by a small, paved road. Their property was one of the houses that was quite large for the two of them, but it was in a nice location, and they liked it. It had a kitchen area and breakfast bar downstairs, along with a lounge, bedroom with en-suite bathroom, and a utility room. Upstairs there were two more bedrooms, a living area, and more bathrooms. Outside at the back and side, there was a small garden that had a patio and a built-in braai, or barbecue, and there was a double garage at the front. It was quite cosy, and they enjoyed living there because it was secure and the neighbours were friendly.

The next thing they had to do was buy a car. They had seen one that Lucy liked very much, a BMW Z3 sports car, in a garage quite close to the house, but when Harry sat in it, his head was touching the roof of the car, so it was too small. His hair was already going thin on the top of his head, and he feared that if he drove that car, it would not be long before the rest of his hair disappeared as well. His friend's son, whom Harry had known since he was a little boy, looked on his laptop and found a few cars that looked good. They saw a BMW 320i which they liked very much so the son drove them over to the garage which had the car for sale, and they had a test drive in it. It was really nice and in very good condition, considering it was already seven years old; the mileage was not too high, either. The price was very reasonable, so they decided to buy it, but this proved more difficult than they had anticipated. Harry did not have a South African bank account at that time and only had a UK bank debit card, so it was a case of trying to transfer money from his UK bank account (which had a limit on daily transactions) to the second-hand car dealer's account. It took a few days but everything was finally completed, and they took possession of the car. They were mobile at last, even though he did not have a South African driving licence or insurance at that time. Things were starting to take shape—or at least that was what they thought, but worse was to come.

Whilst they were waiting to move into the office, they decided one weekend that they would drive down to the Low Veldt, where Harry was interested in visiting one of the Boer War battle scenes called Spion Kop, not far from Ladysmith. They found a nice little guest house on the internet called Easby Guesthouse, which was situated very close to Spion Kop, and booked a room there for the weekend. When they arrived, they discovered that the house and the couple who owned it were very interesting. The house itself, which was built in 1897 on 300 acres of land, had been the headquarters of General Louis Botha in 1899 during the 118-day siege of Ladysmith, from where the Boer defences on the Tugela ridge had been conducted. After the siege was lifted and Ladysmith was relieved, the same house was used by General Sir George White as the British headquarters.

The view from the house over the Northern and Central Drakensburg mountains was amazing. The man, who owned it with his wife, was an ex-history teacher, and his favourite subject was the Boer War. He regaled them each evening they were there with stories about what had happened in that area during various battles of the Boer War. He even offered to take them to the top of Spion Kop in his four-wheel drive vehicle, but Harry thought it was too much to ask of him. The food they served was very homely, and Harry and Lucy shared the same table for their evening meals; they were the only guests. Dinner was followed by coffee as they sat around the blazing fire after dinner, listening to all the owner's stories. Breakfast was served on the thirty-metre-long veranda, which overlooked the open veldt. It was absolutely spectacular and incredibly peaceful to sit there each morning, having a full English breakfast with the sun shining just enjoying the view of the Drakensburg Mountains miles away in the distance, with nothing but open space in between.

It was a very special weekend as far as Harry was concerned. They drove up to the top of Spion Kop to look at where the battle had taken place and looked at the mass grave of the 243 British soldiers who had lost their lives there, as well as the graves of some the 68 Boers on the other side of the Kop who had also died. It was somewhere Harry had wanted to see for a long time after reading various books on the Boer War, but it made him feel quite sad, when he was actually there, to think about all the lives that had been lost simply because of the geographical location of this small hill—and to some extent the stupidity of the officers in charge of the British forces.

Whilst they were down there, the number plate on the front of their car kept falling down; it had been attached with double-sided sticky tape. Harry took it off completely so that they would not lose it altogether and tried to find somewhere where they could have it fixed. He eventually found a small garage, and they fitted it back on for him. He wished afterwards that he hadn't bothered, because a couple of weeks later he received a speeding fine through the post with a picture of the front of the car which clearly showed the number plate, and it had happened just after the number plate had been refitted.

A couple of weeks later, they decided that they should drive to Kruger Park for a weekend. Kruger Park was a game reserve that was about the same size in area as Wales in the UK. It was famous for all of its wild animals roaming free, including elephants, lions, rhinos, leopards, giraffes, buffalos, cheetahs, and a host of other animals. July was the best time to go there because it was winter, and the grasses were quite short, so it made it easier to see the animals. Harry had booked a round, thatched chalet in Oliphants Camp which overlooked the river where animals came to drink in the evenings.

They left Pretoria in the late morning and set off on the five-hour drive to the park, arriving there at about 4.00 PM. When they arrived at the park, the lady at the gate said that there was not sufficient time for them to reach Oliphants Camp before it got dark, so she was not going to allow them to enter. Harry had forgotten just how big the park was—the drive from the gate to their camp was going to take another four hours or so, because of the speed limit in the park. They were really disappointed and thought they would have to find a hotel somewhere where they could stay the night. But thankfully, after checking her computer, the lady came up with a solution. She said that they could stay the first night in Pretorius Camp, which was only about a one-hours drive from the gate, and then they could drive up to Oliphants the next morning. Whilst they were very grateful for her help in finding them somewhere to stay in the camp, Harry was annoyed with himself for not remembering from his previous visit to the Kruger Park just how big it was. Their disappointment was short-lived, however, because within a matter of fifteen minutes of entering the park they saw some cars parked at the side of the road, which was always a good sign that there was some animal not too far away, and there was—a leopard. What a thrill it was to see one so soon after they had arrived. The big cat was relaxing in the afternoon sun in the grass under a tree about thirty yards from the road, walking around every so often and then lying down again. They were excited and thought it was a fantastic start to their visit. They sat in the car for a while and watched it whilst Lucy was taking some photographs, and then they set off again to reach the campsite before they closed the gates for the night.

When they arrived at Pretorius Camp, they were given directions to get to their chalet. It was okay but not much to write home about. Still, at least it was clean and the beds were comfortable. The only trouble was the toilets and bathrooms were some distance away, so Harry had to escort Lucy to the ladies' room, using his torch and waiting outside whilst she did her ablutions before bed.

The next morning they set off for Oliphants Camp. They left quite early because early morning was the best time to see the animals, before they took their afternoon siestas. They were in no rush to get there and so drove quite slowly, keeping their eyes peeled for any animals that might be wandering about the area. It wasn't long before they spotted a herd of elephants heading in their direction. What a magnificent sight! Harry stopped the car, and they sat quietly as the elephants crossed the road a few yards in front of them. There must have been about ten of them altogether, with a baby elephant following its mother bringing up the rear.

A few miles further along the road, where the road crossed over a river, they saw a group of hippos in the water. One minute they could see their heads on the surface, and the next minute they were gone as they dipped under the water. The trip was turning out to be quite spectacular. They were counting down the big five animals, wondering whether they would see them all during their weekend in the park. Before they reached the camp, which was situated in the north side of the park, they saw a lot more animals, including giraffes, kudus, thousands of impala, water buffalo, zebras, and lots of different kinds of birds, some of them very large.

When they arrived at the camp, their round, thatched chalet, with the ensuite bathroom and toilet was perfect. It was on a hillside overlooking the river with a fantastic view of the open bush at the other side. They quickly unpacked their little suitcases and headed to the camp shop to buy some food so that they could have a braai (BBQ) that evening. Harry was a little bit naughty because the braai outside their chalet seemed to be broken, so he swapped it with the one from the chalet next door, which was unoccupied at that time. In the evening after they had eaten their dinner, they sat on the veranda and watched all the animals going down to the river for a drink. What a wonderful, peaceful, and relaxing evening it was, sitting there together and enjoying the view and the activity in the river below—and most of all simply being with each other. It was perfect.

The next morning shortly after the gates of the camp opened at 5.30 AM, they started their drive out of the camp, ready to return to Pretoria. On the way back to the gate, they were keeping their eyes peeled for any animals that might be within view from the road. They were not expecting to see what they did, though. After driving for about an hour, they saw some cars parked with everyone looking into the bush. To their amazement there were three rhinos about half a mile away. It looked as though one of them was a female and the other two were males, because two of them were fighting each other, charging one another with their horns lowered. These animals are enormous and must have weighed a few tons each. Harry imagined being charged by one of them—they could probably turn a bus over if they charged one. They were fighting for quite a while, charging each other repeatedly before one of them finally gave up and wandered away. Not long afterwards, as Harry and Lucy were about halfway in their drive to the gate, they saw another group of cars with everyone peering to the right of the road and wondered what it could be. What a magnificent sight it was. There was a fully grown male lion lying under a tree, taking in the morning sunshine; he was probably resting after having been out hunting and eating all night long. He wasn't very active, probably because he had a full belly, but he did get up from time to time and stretch his legs before lying down again. They watched him for quite a while, with Lucy taking lots of photographs, before they decided that they had best get moving if they were to arrive back in Pretoria at a reasonable time. What a weekend it had been. It was the first time Lucy had seen lots of these animals, and she was excited. They decided that if they ever went again, they would take a private game drive with a guide in one of the campsite's four-wheel-drive, open-top vehicles so that they could get off the road completely and into the bush and be much closer to the animals.

They returned to Pretoria late on the Sunday afternoon and moved into the office the following day, looking forward to getting the business up and running and making some money. They had only been in there a few days when they found out, much to their horror, that the visa collection centre was going to move from their present location to a different suburb some two or three miles away. What a nuisance that was going to be.

As soon as they moved, Harry had some flyers printed and had someone go to the new centre every morning to hand out flyers to potential clients, informing them of his company's presence and location. This worked okay for a couple of weeks, and he did receive inquiries from a couple of clients, but then the girl who had been doing this for him was told that she was not going to be allowed to hand out flyers in that area anymore. On top of this, Harry received a phone call from the leasing agent for the office saying that his so-called friend, his South African partner, had decided to cancel the lease agreement on the office. He would have to move out at the end of the month. She also cancelled the phone contract into which he had just entered. With friends like this, who needed enemies! As soon as he heard the news, he and Lucy jumped into their car and drove over to where the new collection centre was located. They were extremely lucky to meet up with the office complex supervisor, who showed them a small, vacant office that was in an absolutely perfect position because anyone who wanted to submit a UK visa application had to walk past this office in order to get to the VFS collection centre. What a fantastic location! They contacted the leasing company, and a couple of weeks later, before the contract on their existing office expired, they were able to move into the new office. It was a godsend.

It took a little while for them to get everything set up, including the phone and fax lines and the Internet connection, but it was well worth the effort. They started to receive clients almost immediately, which was good, especially after they had wasted five months since their arrival. Lucy accompanied Harry into the office every day and acted as the receptionist. She sat in the outer office looking very beautiful, and Harry would sit in the inner office. He was surprised and very proud of her when he listened to her talking to potential clients and heard how much she knew about visa applications. She never ceased to amaze him and was an amazing girl. She was a real asset, and he was pretty sure that some people used to walk in just because they saw a very beautiful Chinese girl sitting there. Business started picking up, and they were finally making some money at long last without having to rely on Harry's savings.

Shortly after they had moved into the new office, Lucy contacted her old tutor from her master's degree at Leeds University to ask him about the possibilities of her doing her PhD under his supervision. She decided that she would like to research South African investment in China. Her old tutor seemed quite interested in this unique topic and asked her to fly to the UK to meet him so that they could discuss this face to face. Lucy flew to the UK in November using her spouse visa, but when she arrived in the UK, she had problems at the immigration desk at Heathrow Airport. The immigration officer asked her where her husband was, and when she told them Harry was in South Africa, she was detained for an hour and asked a lot of questions. Finally after she had convinced them that she was only visiting the UK briefly to talk to her old tutor about starting a PhD, they allowed her to leave the airport and catch the train up to Leeds. Harry had already booked her hotel accommodation at the Jury's Inn, which was quite close to their old apartment.

She met with her old tutor the following day, and they discussed her proposed subject matter. He agreed to accept her as one of his PhD students, which was great. Lucy was so pleased to be accepted and to be studying once again. She was a very dedicated student and worked extremely hard in anything she did, be it work or studies. When she returned to South Africa a week later, they immediately started looking on the Internet for an apartment which they could rent in Leeds in a similar location to where they had lived before. They found a one-bedroom apartment that looked very nice and clean, and they decided that it would be perfect for her needs. Lucy would be in the UK on her own, and Harry would remain in South Africa running his business. There were three reasons behind this decision. The first was that Lucy needed to live in the UK for twenty-three months in order to qualify for her indefinite leave to remain, and then a further year after that before she got her British citizenship and could apply for a British passport. Her three-year PhD research would cover this period perfectly. The second reason was that she would eventually, after three years, become a doctor, and the third reason was that Harry wanted her to be able to mix with people of her own age for a while—all of his friends in South Africa were of a similar age to him, so it would be good if Lucy had some friends of her own age. At least then he would not feel as though he was depriving her of her youth and keeping her all to himself. It was a win-win situation as far as he was concerned. He would remain in South Africa to keep on working so that he could pay for Lucy's accommodation and living expenses. Lucy had said that her mother, who had finally left her father, was going to sell their apartment in Tianjin and would use that money to pay for her tuition fees, which were quite hefty—GBP30,000 over three years of research. Harry did not realize that her mother's apartment was worth so much money, but the money, wherever it came from, was made available for Lucy's fees.

Lucy Starts her PhD

On 17 December 2009 they travelled to the UK together so that Lucy could have her spouse visa stamped on entry, which meant that the clock would start ticking for her indefinite leave to remain application. They stayed in Jury's Inn for the first night and then went to the real estate company the following morning to pay the deposit and collect the keys to the apartment. They didn't have so much stuff to move, just the two suitcases which they had brought with them from South Africa. The apartment was fully furnished, in any case. It was quite a nice apartment, but something they hadn't realised from the pictures on the Internet was that the apartment was overlooking the intersection of a busy main road with some traffic lights to control the flow of traffic. The noise from outside was much louder than they had expected it to be. Lucy said she did not mind so much and was sure that she would get used to it after living in China for so long. Besides, she would not be in the apartment very much during the day because she would be in university. They moved in the following day and started to get telephone lines, TV channels, and Internet connection installed.

The following day they met up with Harry's sister and her husband, and his cousin for lunch. It was nice for his sister and husband to see Lucy again, and his cousin and for his wife to meet her for the first time. They were impressed with her, and he was proud of how easily she coped with meeting new people. For Christmas Day they bought lots of food from Marks and Spencer and had Christmas lunch at home together. It was nice to be together in the UK, and Harry felt as though he had brought Lucy to her future permanent home.

A couple of days later, they took the train over to East Yorkshire so that Harry could introduce Lucy to his long-standing friend Squire, who had been his best friend for over fifty years. Squire met them at the railway station and was delighted to meet Lucy at long last; Harry had told him so much about her beforehand, when he had seen him during the time he was getting divorced from his ex-wife. Squire lived in a little village called Nafferton just outside of Driffield, where Harry's ex-wife lived. They first went to his house to introduce Lucy to Squire's wife before going down to the local pub for lunch. With Driffield being the gossip centre of the Wolds and surrounding villages, Harry knew that it would not be long before word reached his ex-wife that he had taken his new wife to meet Squire. In fact when Harry spoke to his daughter, Joanne, a couple of weeks later, she told him that they had 'been seen in Driffield'. Harry was not worried in the slightest because he was so proud of Lucy and so much in love with her, and he wanted everyone to see them together and to see how happy they were.

Frequent Flyers

On 2 January he returned to South Africa and left Lucy in Leeds to start her PhD research. It was heart-wrenching to leave her behind again, especially because they had been so happy together in South Africa, but they both knew that it was for the best. She would eventually get her British citizenship and a PhD, so the separation from each other would be worth it in the long run.

Business in South Africa was really picking up, and Harry was busy in the office each day. Lucy was also busy in Leeds preparing herself for starting her PhD research in February. She was going to the university library each day and doing her own research on her chosen topic so that she would be fully prepared for when she started her research in earnest. They were both feeling quite lonely, and Lucy phoned Harry at least four times per day and sent him a long e-mail every evening so that he would have it when he went into the office the next morning. It wasn't the same as being together, but at least they kept in regular contact with one another. Her mails were always very interesting because she told him everything that she had been doing during the day—even down to how many cups of coffee and nibbles she'd had whilst she was at university. Her mails and her phone calls really cheered him up. They had developed their own double talk language, and every time he read it in her e-mail or when they spoke on the phone, he smiled. She would say that she would give him a call call or that she was going to the café for a drink drink, or she was going to the shops to have a look look for any special offers. It was typical of Lucy; she was such a wonderful and funny girl. He loved her so much and looked forward to her phone calls and e-mails every day.

She started her PhD in February 2009 and was relieved to finally get started. Her supervisor thought very highly of her and was pleased to be involved with her again after she had done so well with her master's degree. He listened to what she was planning to do and made some suggestions how she should go about it, which involved various field trips to both South Africa and China. Harry and Lucy were a little bit concerned about Lucy being charged overseas student fees for her research, especially because she had maintained links with the UK whilst they had been away by keeping her UK bank account open. They checked on the Internet and discovered that she should be eligible to apply for UK fees, which were a third of the overseas student fees. They wrote to the university student office giving their reasons why they thought that Lucy qualified for UK fees, but the lady who responded to their letter was adamant that Lucy should pay the overseas student fees. They therefore contacted the student advisory body in London, which was of a similar opinion to Harry and Lucy, but they also said that it was entirely up to the university to decide this matter. Harry and Lucy took legal advice, and their lawyer wrote a few letters to the university, but they were not prepared to budge one inch and maintained that Lucy should pay overseas student fees. Lucy really resented this, but there was nothing they could do about it. They just had to pay up.

Lucy flew out to South Africa in March for a couple of weeks, and they had a lovely time together. Harry was in his element; it was so good to see her and be with her again, and he couldn't keep his hands or eyes off her and wanted to be touching her all the time. He was working in the office most days and had a receptionist, so Lucy did not need to go into the office each day; she was happy to stay at home working on her studies. They did manage a few days away together, especially because there was a South African holiday during her visit. They also went to a very nice French restaurant in Pretoria called La Madeleine, which Harry used to frequent during the mid-1980s when he was working at the British embassy in Pretoria. It was still owned by the same man, but it had moved from the centre of town into one of the suburbs because it was not particularly safe at night to be wandering around the centre of Pretoria these days. The owner of the restaurant always amused Harry every time he went because once his guests were seated, he would come over and tell his customers what was on the menu that evening. It was just like listening to Rene from the 'Allo 'Allo comedy programme on the TV. Harry felt sure that it was a put-on, exaggerated French accent, but nevertheless it was funny. The food there was always excellent, albeit a bit expensive. Lucy discovered that they had some Normandy Cider, which she particularly liked, and she even asked if they could buy a case from them. Unfortunately they didn't have enough to spare, but they promised to get her a case for the next time.

They met up with some old friends of Harry's whom Lucy had met before whilst she was living with him in Pretoria. They were always pleased to see her and thought the world of her.

Harry used to go around to their house to watch rugby quite a lot whilst he was on his own, and they were invited again, this time whilst Lucy was visiting. Harry and his friend Des watched the rugby match whilst his wife, Helene, and Lucy were busy in the kitchen preparing the salad and dessert that they would have with their braai, which Des would cook after the game was over. Des was a real expert with the braai. Lucy and Helene got on extremely well together, and their laughter could be heard whilst Harry and Des were watching the game. Lucy would pop out of the kitchen from time to time so that Harry could have a kiss and a cuddle, which was always very welcome. He could never get enough of her; just looking at her and holding her and kissing her made him feel like the luckiest man alive.

Lucy returned to the UK at the end of her visit, and they were already planning when they would see each other again and where it would be. Shortly after Lucy had gone back, the landlord of the house Harry was renting decided that he was going to move back into his property and wanted them to vacate the property. It came as a bit of a shock not only because they still had a couple of months on the tenancy agreement, but also because they had been very happy there. A couple of weeks later the leasing agent contacted Harry again to say that the landlord had changed his mind, and they could stay. That was a huge relief, but it was short lived. A few weeks later the agent contacted Harry yet again and said that the landlord had changed his mind a second time and would like to move back into his property. Harry had started to make inquiries about finding another apartment when the agent phoned him again to say that, again, the landlord had changed his mind. This was crazy. Whilst Harry was happy to be staying there, he did not want to be living on a knife's edge. He decided that it was probably best if he found somewhere else for them to live. As it worked out, it was a good decision because the landlord changed his mind once again and decided that he really did want to move back into his house. That was fine with Harry—he had already found another apartment that was closer to his office, so he moved out before the lease expired.

The new apartment which he had found was in Brooklyn and was in a large, six-floor apartment block which stood in its own ground with a high wall and electric fences of top of it. The apartment itself was on the first floor and was quite large. It had a large kitchen, a dining area, a lounge, a small TV room, two bedrooms, and two bathrooms. The outlook from the balcony, which overlooked the front of the property and the beautifully maintained gardens, was very nice indeed. The lady who owned the apartment was a divorcee and was retired. She had decided that she wanted to travel the world for a couple of years during her twilight years and would use the rent from her apartment to help to pay for her travel. When Harry saw the apartment at first, it was fully furnished with all of her belongings, but when he told her he already had a double bed, a settee, and a TV, she put quite a bit of her stuff into storage or into the garage on the ground floor. He also had a three-seater swing and a braai, which he put on the balcony. Lucy and he had loved sitting on the swing (or as she called it, the swing swing) together in their old house, so it was a nice reminder of her every evening when he sat on it.

The apartment was a nice place to live, but the man who had taken over the responsibility of warden of the complex was becoming a bit of a nuisance. He really kept an eye on everything and ruled the apartment block with an iron first. Harry had brought his charcoal braai with him, which in a way was a South African culture. But when he lit it for the first time, the warden came around and knocked at the door, telling him that he could not use a braai in the apartment block. Harry thought this was a bit strange because the person in the next apartment to him, whose balcony was next to his, used to have a braai every weekend. He pointed this out to the warden, and he said that gas or electric braais were allowed but not charcoal, because they gave off smoke. Harry therefore decided that he would buy a gas braai before Lucy came out again.

In July he flew back to the UK again to see Lucy, and they had arranged that they would meet in London so that they could enjoy some shopping and go to see a couple of shows. He had arrived early in the morning and dropped off his bags at the guest house where they would be staying in Bloomsbury, which was not far from Kings Cross, where Lucy would be arriving later that morning. He could not wait to see her and was waiting at the station a long time before the train arrived. She had sent him a text message and called his mobile phone to say that she was on the way and could not wait to see him again. He felt exactly the same—he was wishing the time away and hoping that the train would arrive early. The train eventually did arrive on time, and he anxiously waited for her to walk down the platform. It seemed that everyone else on the train had walked through the ticket barrier, but there was still no sign of her. He was beginning to feel worried, but finally he saw her, and his heart nearly exploded with the excitement of seeing her again. He could not wait to hold her and look at her and be with her again. They spent a few minutes holding and kissing each other before they finally picked up her bags and walked to the guest house. It was not a special place, but they knew that they would only be sleeping there and would spend most of the days and evenings outside.

They had planned that they would see a couple of musicals whilst they were there, and they had decided the best way to get good seats was to go straight to the theatre box office to see if they had any cancellations for the show that evening. They had been really lucky a few times in the past doing this, when they lived in Wapping, and they had been able to get some excellent seats at the last minute, within five or six rows of the stage. They decided that they would like to see *Chicago* the first night, and on the second night they saw *Dreamboats and Petticoats*, which was all 1950s music—Harry's era. The seats they got for each of the shows were not as good as they had hoped, but they were not bad.

They spent the rest of the day shopping in the West End and had lunch in a nice little French restaurant which had tables outside on the pavement. The place was packed, which was hardly surprising once they tasted the food; the staff were very friendly and the service was excellent. They had opted to sit outside and had a light lunch because they knew that they would be having dinner before the show started. It was wonderful to be with Lucy again. Being with her always made Harry feel so happy and reminded him of why he loved her so much.

That evening they had dinner in an Italian restaurant just off Trafalgar Square, where Lucy had first met Joanne a couple of years before. The food in that restaurant was always good even though the service sometimes left a little bit to be desired. They didn't really care, though, because they were happy to be together and were looking forward to the show afterwards, which was excellent. Once the show was over, they walked back hand in hand to their little guest house.

The following morning, they decided that rather than have breakfast in the guest house, they would go to an Italian café which was a five-minute walk away. Lucy had been there before on one of her visits to London to attend a seminar with her supervisor. It was really good, and the coffee was excellent as was the food. The lady who served them had been really grumpy at first, but she became much more friendly towards them as she got to know them over the years they went there. The food and the coffee never disappointed.

The next day was very similar to the first day. They went shopping for most of the day and had lunch in the Japanese restaurant in Harvey Nichols. That evening they had dinner in the Italian restaurant off Trafalgar Square again because it was really close to the theatre where *Dreamboats and Petticoats* was playing. They sat outside this time at a table on the pavement and enjoyed a bottle of wine along with their meal. Then they sat there just enjoying being together and watching all the people walking by. The show was excellent, and it was fun to watch lots of old ladies who were getting up and dancing in the aisles. They could see one group of ladies who were sitting in a box very close to the stage and really getting into the swing of it all; they were dancing and singing throughout the show. It was a lovely evening, and Lucy really enjoyed it. They walked back to the guest house again and stopped off for a drink on the way back.

The following day they caught the train up to Leeds because Lucy had to attend a meeting with her supervisor. Harry also had a few things to do in Leeds, so they were both pretty busy once they got back home.

On Saturday they met up with Harry's sister and her husband, as well as his cousin and his wife for lunch. Harry's cousin, who was a few years older than him, had taken a real shine to Lucy after his first meeting with her, and after the lunch was over, he took everyone back to his house, where he dug out his bright yellow Teddy Boy jacket to show Lucy. It was a fingertip drape jacket with a black collar and black on the top of each half-moon pocket. He really looked the part when he put it on—albeit a lot older than he had been when he was a Teddy Boy in his teens and early 20's. He was telling Lucy that he still went to Teddy Boy reunions, which were held in different pubs where everyone dresses up in the 1950s style. Lucy was telling him how much she had enjoyed the show *Dreamboats and Petticoats*; she also told him about the time she went into a supermarket in Leeds to try to buy a bottle of wine. They refused to serve her because they thought she was underage and did not have any identification. She said she had been fuming at the time, but Harry told her that she should be flattered if they thought she was still a teenager.

That evening they went out for dinner to an Indian restaurant not far from the apartment. It was going to be their last dinner together for a little while because Harry was flying back to South Africa the following day. It was always difficult to leave Lucy, and he hated doing so, but they both knew that he needed to work to pay for her apartment and living expenses. It didn't make it any easier for them, though, and although they had a lovely evening together, it was in the back of their minds that he would have to leave the next morning. It was even more a pity because it was the day before his birthday. He would arrive back in South Africa to spend his birthday alone but with memories of his last week with Lucy in the UK. Lucy was not really into buying cards for birthdays or Christmas, and Harry had never received a card from her all the time they had been together even though he sent her cards for her birthday, Valentine's Day, Christmas, and anniversaries. She teased him one year because he had sent her a card for their wedding anniversary that was identical to the one he had sent her the year before. She accused him of being a Yorkshire man—careful with his money—and said that he must have bought a job lot of identical cards, or at least a box full of them. He told her that it was the words in the card that had attracted him towards it, not the card itself, and that his love and devotion for her expressed in the words in the card was still the same and still as strong as ever.

A few weeks after he arrived back in South Africa, Lucy phoned Harry to say that she had seen a part-time job advertised on the university noticeboard for someone who could speak Chinese and had good computer skills. The company which had placed the advertisement was a large international company with offices in Leeds, London, and other cities around the world, including Japan. They were interested in developing their business in China and needed a Chinese-speaking person to help them with this. She was really excited at the prospect of being able to work and earn some money of her own, even though Harry was sending her spending money every month from South Africa. She went for the interview and was absolutely delighted when she heard a few days later that she had got the job. They wanted her to work two days per week. which fitted in perfectly with her research, and they would pay her a very good salary—around GBP1,000 per month after tax. She was over the moon because not only would she be gaining some valuable work experience, but she would also have some money of her own to buy clothes and other things she wanted, without having to ask Harry for the money.

She started work for the company a couple of weeks later at the beginning of the next month, and it didn't take her long to settle in and to get to know what was required of her. From what she told Harry, her job was to find out what the populations were in various cities around China and to find out what companies were there so that this information could be sold to other companies who were thinking of investing in China or who were already there. One of the companies who wanted information about China was Adidas. It was strange in a way because one of Lucy's former colleagues from the Chinese company she had worked for in Beijing had joined Adidas in a very senior position and was working at their office in Shanghai. Another girl whom Lucy knew also worked for Adidas, and she had previously worked for Harry in his office in Beijing. It was a small world.

Her new employers were amazed at how many contacts she had in China, and no doubt they could not believe their luck at finding such a talented and well-connected young lady. They had previously been buying all this kind of information from Chinese companies or American universities, but once Lucy started working for them, they were able to get this information much easier and without having to pay exorbitant fees for it. Lucy even had a friend in China who worked for the Chinese government and was doing something similar, and she used to contact him from time to time if ever she needed something that she could not find out for herself, which was not very often.

Some of her colleagues, who were set in their ways of paying for information from other sources, seemed to resent her ability to find things out. It took her some time to make them realize that there were easier and cheaper ways of doing things. One guy in particular used to resist telling her anything about one particular computer programme which he used to analyse the data, because he knew that she was so clever that she would soon be able to understand it and use it better than he could. Luckily the guy she was directly working for was much nicer, and he enjoyed working with her and realised how much of an asset she was to him, as well as how much easier his life had become in the office since she arrived. It was not long before her personality, skills, and dedication to work won everyone over, and she became accepted by everyone, including some of the directors who had also seen her potential. She was very happy in what she was doing. The two days she worked each week did not interfere with her own research and were pretty flexible, which meant that she was able to decide which days she went into the office depending on her university commitments. She was also meeting different people of her own age away from her university colleagues, which was good, and she was being paid very well for it.

Lucy decided that she would like to visit South Africa again in September because there was a seminar being held in Pretoria on South African business investment in China, which Harry had told her about. She was really excited at the prospect of meeting the man who was the guest speaker at the seminar because she had read some of his books and pamphlets in the university library. Harry booked her flight, and she arranged to have a few days off work. She arrived on 11 September so that she would be fully rested for when the seminar took place on 16 September. Harry was overjoyed at seeing her again as she walked into the arrivals area at the airport in Johannesburg, but he could tell from her face that she was not very happy. He asked her what was wrong, and she told him that she was angry because when she was at the immigration desk, the immigration officer checking her passport had been trying to flirt with her. When she hadn't responded to his advances, he had threatened to not allow her in and was threatening to send her back to China—even though she had arrived from the UK. Harry was very angry to hear this and started searching for the immigration office so that he could report this to the head of the immigration service at the airport. Everyone he asked did not seem to know where he was and was not that interested in any case. He tried for a good twenty minutes before Lucy decided that it was not worth the effort, and they drove home together.

It was lovely for Harry to have her home again, especially because it was the first time that she had been to the new apartment. She liked it very much, especially the little TV room, which also had bookshelves and a table and chair where she could work on her university research whilst Harry was in the office. The night after she arrived, they decided that they would use the gas braai on the balcony and have a braai for dinner. They had been shopping for meat and salad ingredients after Harry got home from the office, and they were really looking forward to using the braai and sitting on the swing swing together to eat it. Harry lit the braai and left it to warm up before putting a nice round of boerewors, a South African sausage, on to cook. It smelled wonderful, but there was a little bit of smoke coming from the fat leaking onto the flames from the sausage as it cooked. Within a matter of minutes of this happening, a voice shouted up from the garden complaining about the smoke. It was the apartment complex warden saying that someone had complained to him about all the smoke coming from the balcony. It really annoyed Harry, who told him that he was using a gas braai, as he had been told, and that it was just the fat from the boerewors causing the smoke. The warden told him to be more careful, which resulted in Harry swearing at him and telling him that a braai was part of South African culture and that he was sick of him always coming around to complain each time he lit the braai—especially because this was Lucy's first braai in the new apartment. They continued with the braai and enjoyed eating the food on the swing swing, but the confrontation with the warden had taken the edge of their enjoyment.

The night of the seminar arrived, and Harry drove Lucy to the venue, which was at a large Volkswagen garage a few miles away. They arrived in plenty of time and had a glass of wine in the conference area before the seminar started. Harry didn't really understand much of what was said, but Lucy said that she had found it very interesting and helpful. At the end of the seminar, she introduced herself to the speaker and had a long conversation with him about what she was doing in the UK. He was really impressed and promised to send her some of his writings and books that she had not read. She was thrilled to bits, not only to have met him but for him to be so kind. It really had been worth her while to come out. She stayed on for a couple of more days, during which time she made a lot of notes about what had been said at the seminar; she used her fantastic memory to write almost word for word what the speaker had said.

In November there was another forum arranged at the Pretoria Business School complex in Johannesburg, which Lucy said she would also like to attend. There was a hotel within the business complex, and Harry booked a room for the two of them so that they could stay there when Lucy arrived, the evening before the Forum took place. Harry checked into the hotel in the afternoon when he finished work and went to the airport to collect Lucy when her flight arrived later that evening. As he was driving to the airport a couple of hours before the flight arrived, he realised what a dodgy area it was. He had heard lots of reports of drivers who had stopped at red lights and had been robbed at gunpoint or had their cars stolen, especially when it was dark, and he was beginning to wonder if there was an alternative route back to the hotel, especially when he would be carrying his precious passenger. Harry arrived at the airport in plenty of time and started asking other people whether they knew of a different route back to the hotel. One guy suggested that if he was worried about driving back the same way he had come, he should just drive up the freeway to Pretoria and then take the N1 freeway to Johannesburg. It was not a good idea.

Lucy arrived safe and sound and without any problems at the immigration desk this time. For Harry it was lovely to see her again, as always, and they quickly wheeled her little suitcase to the car and set off for the hotel, taking the same route as he had taken to get to the airport. His senses were on high alert as he was driving, and he was watching everything in front of the car, at the sides, and also behind. Whenever they came to a traffic light which was red, he ignored it and drove straight through. He could not risk anything happening to them, especially to Lucy, who was the most important person in the world to him. Thankfully they reached the hotel without any problems and managed to get a snack before going to bed.

The following morning after breakfast, Harry drove back up to Pretoria to work in his office all day; he left Lucy in the business school so that she could attend the forum when it started later that morning. Lunch was going to be provided, so he knew that she would be okay during the day. He returned to Johannesburg to collect her later in the afternoon, after he had finished with his clients; she was waiting for him because the forum had finished slightly earlier than expected. She had really enjoyed it, and it had provided her with lots of useful information and given her lots of new ideas that she could incorporate into her research.

They drove back to the apartment in Pretoria that evening to prepare for her attending another seminar on Friday evening. Lucy was busy making notes from the previous forum and researching information about the person who was presenting the next seminar. They did have time to relax together and do some shopping together to the local Spar shop. One of the guys who worked there was forever asking Harry, when he went shopping there on his own, where his wife was and when she was coming out again. He was pleased to see her this time when they went. She had an effect on people; it was almost a case of once seen, never forgotten, which was how Harry felt about her the first time he saw her. It was not only her beauty but her whole demeanour that attracted people towards her.

The Chamber of Commerce in Pretoria had organised the seminar on the Friday, so it was not too far to travel. They had been to other seminars at this location and knew how to get there. They arrived in plenty of time so that they would have time to have some nibbles and a glass of wine before it started. Lucy enjoyed it very much and chatted with the speaker afterwards. He was also very interested in her research topic and offered to help her in any way he could.

On Sunday Harry's daughter, Joanne, arrived in South Africa on a business trip for her employers in Holland. She was staying with Harry and Lucy Sunday and Monday night before flying down to Cape Town on Tuesday for more business meetings. They both went to the airport to pick her up on the Sunday evening and drove back to the apartment. Lucy and Harry were both pleased to see her, especially because she had brought some of their favourite cake and cheese from Holland. Harry was working the next day and his daughter was attending meetings, but he had arranged that they all go out for dinner with Des and Helene, whom Joanne had not seen since she had visited South Africa from boarding school in the UK, over twenty years before. He booked a table at an Italian restaurant which Helene recommended, and it was not too far from their apartment.

With it being a Monday evening, the restaurant was very quiet, and they had the place to themselves. As usual Des and

Helene were late, but Harry, Lucy, and Joanne entertained themselves and had a drink until they arrived. It was a real reunion atmosphere. Des and Helene had not seen Lucy for a little while, and they had not seen Joanne since she was a schoolgirl. Needless to say, the conversation and laughter went on all evening, and not one them could remember much about the food, only that they had all had a really good time and it was nice for everyone to meet up again after so long.

Joanne left the following morning for Cape Town, and Lucy and Harry had a few days on their own before Lucy also had to leave on Friday. One evening they had a Chinese banquet, which Lucy prepared. She was an excellent cook and watched lots of cookery programmes on the TV, which meant that she could cook all different kinds of dishes from many different countries. Her mother thought that she couldn't cook at all, but she didn't know how good Lucy really was. Her Chinese food was delicious—in fact it was better than her mother's, although Harry would never tell her mother that. She must have watched her mother for years and years, and knowing what a fantastic brain she had, she took everything in and stored it for later use.

Lucy left on Friday evening, and they resumed their daily contact with each other by e-mail and telephone. She continued to phone about five times per day to let Harry know what she was doing and also to find out what he had been doing. She would phone him as soon as she opened her eyes every morning and talk to him with a very sleepy voice. He loved these calls and wished he could be there to look at her when she opened her eyes each morning. He loved waking her up with a kiss when they were together, and he liked to see her peeping out from underneath the duvet cover. She always looked so beautiful.

Christmas Holiday

In December Lucy flew out to South Africa again to spend Christmas and New Year with Harry. She arrived on 15 December, and after a visit to the beautician, where she had her nails done and a massage, they had a few days relaxing at home before they were ready on 20 December for their Christmas holiday trip to Cape Town and Stellenbosch. Harry had booked their holiday some months in advance to make sure that they managed to get the holiday they had been dreaming about.

On 20 December they took a taxi to the railway station in Pretoria, where they were catching the Blue Train to Cape Town. The Blue Train was like a mobile five-star hotel, a bit like the Orient Express in Europe. They had their own cabin for sleeping with an en-suite bathroom and toilet, and all the five-star cuisine was served in the dining car. There was also a bar where all the drinks, snacks, and cigars were free. When they arrived at the railway station, they were shown into the Blue Train departure lounge, and Champagne and other drinks were available along with some very nice finger foods. Their bags were whisked away by someone, and they waited to board with their hand baggage. As soon as everything was ready, they had been greeted by the person in charge of the Blue Train in Pretoria; he made a very nice welcoming speech and described the history of the Blue Train and told everyone what they could expect when they boarded. It was very luxurious. Kings and presidents had travelled on this magnificent, mobile, five-star hotel. The train departed from Pretoria at about 10.00 AM on Monday morning and arrived in Cape Town the following lunchtime. It was not a fast train, but it was nice to be able to relax in such pleasant and comfortable surroundings.

Within a couple of hours of leaving the station, they experienced their first taste of the five-star food on the train when they went for lunch. The service and the food was amazing, and it was hard to believe that with the kitchen being so small, the chefs could prepare food of such a high standard. The waiters were so friendly that it was an absolute pleasure to eat in the dining car. In between meals. Harry and Lucy were either in their little cabin, which was like a little lounge, or in the bar enjoying the free drinks.

The train stopped at Kimberly for an hour, and anyone who wanted to, including Lucy and Harry, were able to take a coach trip to see the Big Hole, which was dug by hand between 1871, when diamonds were first discovered, and 1914, when mining came to an end. Over the period of time it was open, 50,000 minors dug the hole, which measured 463 metres across and 240 metres deep; during this time they dug out 2,720 kilos of diamonds. It is an incredible sight and was hard to believe that a hole so wide and so deep had been dug by miners using picks and shovels. Following their visit, they returned to the train just in time to freshen up and get dressed for dinner. There was a dress code on the train for dinner: men had to wear a suit and tie, and ladies wore a dress. Again the food and service were excellent.

After dinner they had a nightcap in the bar before going back to their cabin, where the lounge had been converted into a bedroom and the bed was made up, ready for them to have a good night's sleep.

Breakfast next morning was delicious, as were the rest of the meals they had had on the train. It was really nice to sit in the dining car eating breakfast and watching the world go by through the window. There had not been very much to see of great of interest as they crossed the Karoo, which was pretty desolate; besides, most of the journey through there had been during the night. But as the train got nearer to the cape, the landscape and the scenery started to change dramatically, and they could see mountains, large wine estates, and fruit farms all over the place. It was amazing how many wine estates and fruit farms they passed—and this was probably only a small proportion of the total in Cape Province. It was a wonderful sight and really whetted their appetites for wine and fruit when they arrived.

The train eventually pulled into the station in Cape Town, and they disembarked after receiving some nice gifts of a miniature gold-plated mantelpiece clocks, one for each of them. Harry was not sure where the car hire office was, but once they got out of the station, there was a man holding a sign waiting for them, and he took them along to the car hire office in the centre of town, where they collected their car and a map. Harry had brought their GPS system with them, so he plugged it into the cigarette lighter and set off for their hotel. They were staying in the Protea Fire and Ice Hotel, which seemed very nice and in a quiet location. After checking in, they went up to their room, which was large and comfortable, to unpack and freshen up before going for a walk to try to get their bearings and see if they could find any places of interest—especially restaurants. Harry had booked to stay in the hotel until Christmas morning, when they would drive up to Stellenbosch to stay on a wine estate there for the last couple of days of their holiday.

That evening they drove down to the Victoria and Alfred waterfront to wander around and to find a nice restaurant where they could sit outside and watch the sun go down. The waterfront was very busy, with it being the summer holiday season in South Africa, and there were lots of tourists and locals wandering around and doing exactly what they were doing—relaxing and enjoying being there. There were lots of different kinds of boat cruises to be had, as well as speed boat rides and trips on yachts and catamarans, but Lucy, who couldn't swim did not really fancy any of those, so they wandered around the shopping mall looking at different shops before selecting a nice restaurant for dinner. Strangely enough, as Harry found out later, they chose the same restaurant that was part of the hotel where his daughter had stayed when she visited Cape Town a couple of months before. She had also had dinner sitting outside and watching all the activity along the dockside.

The next morning after a very nice breakfast in the hotel, they planned to take the cable car to the top of Table Mountain, but when Harry went outside the hotel before breakfast to look at the mountain, to his dismay it was covered in clouds—or as people liked to say, it had its tablecloth on. They kept hoping that the clouds would clear, but they remained there for the whole day. They therefore decided to drive along the coast line to Camps Bay and Hout Bay. Camps Bay was like most seaside resorts, full of small restaurants all the way along the seafront, but Hout Bay was more of a port where fishing boats used to come and go. Needless to say, there were a few fish restaurants there, along with quite a lot of local stalls selling trinkets, carvings, and other souvenirs. Some of them were very interesting, but they did not buy anything because the carvings they particularly liked were quite large and would have been difficult to take back to Pretoria on the flight.

They spent most of the morning relaxing and wandering about in Hout Bay before returning to Camps Bay where they went for a walk along the beach. There were some local children swimming in the sea even though the water looked quite cold. Harry did manage to persuade Lucy to take off her shoes and go for a paddle at the edge of the water. Her face was an absolute picture; it was so cold that she screwed up her face as she half screamed with the cold. But Harry ended up paying the price for laughing: she started to kick water at him, and he ended up getting a little bit wet. As soon as he started doing the same, Lucy announced that she was 'not playing', so they declared a truce and decided that the best thing they could do was to go and have some lunch at one of the restaurants along the sea front.

Lucy, who had a very healthy appetite and generally ate three times more food than Harry—and still managed to remain slim—had an enormous lobster salad; Harry had a steak with salad. Both were very nicely cooked and very well presented. It was such a relaxing lunch—good food with a very beautiful girl and a beautiful sea view. What a great start to their holiday.

After a very leisurely lunch and a lazy afternoon driving around different parts of Cape Town, they returned to the hotel to have a shower and get ready for dinner in a lovely restaurant just opposite the hotel. Harry had met the chef from the restaurant that morning while he had been standing in the road gazing at Table Mountain wishing the clouds to disappear. The chef who was from Scotland had told Harry that the restaurant had only been open a few weeks, and that the menu was really good. He had even shown him around the place and showed him their menu, and Harry agreed that it did look good. There was an open-air veranda area at one side of the restaurant, where guests could sit and have a drink and a smoke before dinner if they so wished; the interior was quite dark, but they had some really subtle lighting that made it a very romantic place to eat—just right for Lucy and Harry. They did not rush their evening and sat on the veranda having a couple of drinks before going inside to order dinner. The food was superb as anticipated, and they really enjoyed their dinner and took their time; there was no rush when he was on holiday with someone he loved as much as he loved Lucy.

The next morning, as was becoming his routine, Harry went down to the restaurant before Lucy was up and about, to have a coffee and to stand in the street, and look at the mountain to see if it was clear. It wasn't. He was beginning to get a little bit worried that they would not be able to go on the cable car to the top whilst they were there. No matter how much he looked at them, the clouds were not moving. He went back up to their room to wake Lucy and to get a shower before they went down to breakfast together, where they discussed what they would do that day. They only had one more day left in Cape Town after this and were hoping that they would be able to get to the top of Table Mountain before they left. They decided that all they could do was to have a walk around town and then go to the waterfront again.

After wandering around for quite a while, they eventually found their way to the waterfront again and went inside the mall to investigate what shops they had there. Window shopping passed a couple of hours for them, and then they decided to have a walk along the waterfront towards the area where some of the larger boats and ships were moored. As they were walking along, a man approached them and offered them a choice of helicopter rides. One of them he said was in an old US Army helicopter, a Huey, which had been used during the Vietnam War. The other was an ordinary commercial kind of helicopter. He told them that the ordinary helicopter was just for sightseeing and would fly all over Cape Town and along the coastline so that they could see everything from the air. The Huey was more of an adventure flight, where it would be swooping, diving, and swerving all over the place, but it would not be a sightseeing trip. After seeing both helicopters, they decided, given that the Huey did not have any doors, they would opt for the ordinary helicopter trip. They paid their money and accompanied the pilot towards the helicopter. They had decided that Lucy should sit in the front alongside the pilot because her camera skills were much better than Harry's. They donned their crash helmets, which had built-in microphones in them so that they could talk to each other and also hear what the pilot had to say as he described what they were flying over. It was a very interesting flight, a first for them.

For the rest of the afternoon, they wandered around the waterfront and watched various people performing African dances as well as other groups of people singing and playing various instruments. It was an enjoyable time, being together and so much in love. After an early dinner in one of the Italian restaurants, they had a slow walk hand in hand back to the hotel.

When they arrived back at the hotel, they saw a sign on the reception desk saying that any guest who wanted to upgrade their room to a small apartment fifty metres down the road from the hotel could do so. This sounded rather grand, and they were very interested and inquired at the desk. One of the receptionists took them along to show them the apartments, which were very comfortable. There was an upstairs and a downstairs. On the ground floor of the apartment was a small kitchen area, a lounge area with settees, and a TV as well as a toilet. The marble stairs at the side of the lounge led up to the bedroom and bathroom area. It was homely, and they decided that they would upgrade their room so that they could spend their last two nights in their own little world. It was wonderful—they could do whatever they liked without fear of anyone hearing or seeing them. They both wandered around half naked, and Lucy, who was just wearing a towel around herself after having a shower, looked very sexy and provocative. Harry started taking some photographs of her as she walked up the stairs to the bedroom wearing her towel, which was falling off, and he eventually persuaded her to allow him to take some photographs of her naked. They turned out really well, and she looked amazing. It was difficult taking photographs of someone he loved as much as he loved Lucy, who was lying naked on the bed looking so beautiful—especially when he was naked himself. One thing led to another, and he put the camera down to join her on the bed to give her his full attention.

Next morning when Harry woke up, he went to get his early morning coffee as was his daily routine. Much to his delight the sky was clear, so he finished his coffee and rushed back to the apartment to wake Lucy and give her the good news. They wanted to get up the mountain as quickly as possible before any clouds arrived again, so after a quick shower they dashed along to the restaurant and had breakfast before they jumped into the car to drive up to the road where the cable car base station was located. There were quite a lot of people waiting, probably because, like Lucy and Harry, they had been waiting a couple of days for the clouds to clear. Eventually after queuing for a little while, they managed to buy their tickets and boarded the cable car. The view from the cable car was fantastic; they could see the whole of Cape Town and the harbour. Lucy took quite a few photographs as the cable car glided up the wire to the top. When they reached the top, the view was even more spectacular. Not only could they see the whole of Cape Town, but they could also see around the coastline, as well as towards Camps Bay and Hout Bay. Whilst the trip for the fantastic view was worth it, there was not a lot to do on the top of Table Mountain. There was a restaurant and a shop selling souvenirs, but that was about all. They wandered around for a little while, and Harry took some photographs of Lucy as a reminder of their trip to the top. Then they decided to catch the cable car down again. Once they reached the bottom, they took a drive to Camps Bay again, where they had lunch. In the late afternoon it was back to the waterfront, and they had dinner there. This was their last evening in Cape Town before they left the next morning to drive to Stellenbosch, where Harry had booked a room in the Spire Hotel, which was also a wine estate. They had a relaxing dinner and sat there afterwards enjoying their coffee and watching the sun go down, happy to be together.

The next morning after a leisurely breakfast, they packed their bags and drove up to Stellenbosch, which was only about forty-five minutes away from Cape Town. It was much hotter there—in the mid to high thirties. They found the hotel, situated a few miles outside of Stellenbosch, without too much trouble and then parked the car and checked in at the reception desk. Once they had checked in, they were driven in a little golf buggy to their room, which turned out to be more like a little townhouse. There were a few rows of little houses with nice, little, narrow streets running between them. Each 'house' had its own entrance and also a small garden in the back. Inside it was just like any other hotel room, with a bathroom and a bedroom and some veranda doors leading to the garden; it was very pleasant and quiet. The house was a three-minute walk from the hotel and the swimming pool. The hotel, which was all on one level, had a large dining area and a large bar area, with the swimming pool next to the dining area.

They had a walk around to get their bearings and then decided to go back to the house to get their swimming things before returning to the pool to do some sunbathing and splash around in the pool. Lucy decided that she would stay in the shallow end whilst Harry swam up and down. A couple of times he swam underwater from the deep end so that she would not see him coming and grabbed her legs, which really surprised her and gave her a shock, but luckily it resulted in him having a hug and kiss in the water. They lazed around the pool on the sunbeds for a little while before going back to their house for a siesta before dinner. They had considered driving into Stellenbosch, but a siesta was more inviting, and in any case with it being Christmas Day, there would not be a lot happening in town.

After they got out of bed, they showered and got dressed for dinner, with Lucy wearing a strapless white dress and a string of pearls around her neck. She looked absolutely fabulous. They strolled over to the hotel and had a couple of drinks in the bar; Lucy had some weird cocktail which looked like a chocolate milkshake but was very alcoholic. The food was good, as they had expected it would be, and they spent a quiet evening sitting around the veranda area of the dining room having coffee and enjoying each other's company in such peaceful surroundings.

The next morning they drove into Stellenbosch, which is a university town, and wandered around there for most of the morning taking in the sights and having coffee in different cafes.

It was pretty quiet because all of the students were away on their summer holidays but there were a few American tourists wandering around but not many local people. Given that it was only one day after Christmas, the quiet was to be expected. Lucy really liked Stellenbosch and started to wonder whether she could transfer her PhD research to Stellenbosch University from Leeds; at least then they would be closer to each other and would be able to see each other more often. It was an attractive idea, but that would not help her to get her British nationality, so they shelved it.

After lunch they returned to the hotel, where they thought they should try the wine tasting. They inquired at the reception desk and were then driven in a little golf buggy along a narrow road that had lots of stalls selling locally produced goods. Soon they arrived at the wine area of the complex, half a mile from the hotel itself. When they got there, they were the only people there and so had the full attention of all the staff, who told them what choices they had for the wine tasting. The lady in charge said that they had two choices: the cheaper choice allowed them a selection of three or four wines to taste, and if they paid a little bit more they could have a selection of six wines. They decided that they would try six. They all tasted very nice, but Lucy particularly liked one of the red wines, so they decided to buy two bottles to take back to Pretoria.

The following day they checked out of the hotel and started their return journey to Cape Town, to catch the flight back to Johannesburg. From there they'd take a taxi to the apartment in Pretoria. They had plenty of time before the flight, and so they decided that they would make a few detours before going to the airport. They drove around some beautiful little places at a leisurely pace before arriving in Somerset West, a place Harry had heard of but had never been to before. He was not really sure what to expect, but it certainly didn't live up to his expectations. It seemed a dirty little place with lots of run-down buildings; maybe they were just in the wrong part of town. Neither of them felt very comfortable walking around, so they thought it best to get back into the car and make their way back to Cape Town. Their holiday was just about over and they returned the car to the car hire company at the airport and caught a flight back to Johannesburg. It had been a wonderful holiday, the best they'd ever had—a belated honeymoon in a way. Lucy loved Cape Town and the surrounding areas, and they promised each other that they would certainly come down again sometime for another visit.

On 29 December, a couple of days after Harry and Lucy arrived back in Pretoria, Lucy left for the UK. It had been a really relaxing holiday for her and had taken her mind off her studies and work for a couple of weeks, which was good. Her batteries were recharged, and she was ready to resume her studies. It had been wonderful for Harry to be with her and spend some quality time together, and they were already making plans on when they would be able to see each other again.

Harry returned to the UK in March so that he could see her again. They met up in London as usual and stayed in a guest house in Bloomsbury, spending a wonderful few days together shopping, eating out, and going to some more shows in the West End. Their time together was so precious to them both that they wanted it to go on forever, but work commitments meant that Harry could only stay for a few days. She also had commitments with her studies and her work, but even just a short time together was worth it.

Lucy flew to China and Singapore at the end of April for a few days to carry out some fieldwork. She had arranged meetings with various South African businessmen in Shanghai and Beijing in connection with her PhD research, and both sets of meetings proved to be very useful to her. Being back in China was a golden opportunity for her to meet up with her mother again for a couple of days; she had not seen her since she'd left in 2009. Lucy was staying in a self-catering apartment in Beijing in a hotel complex, so it was very easy for her mother to stay and to prepare some delicious food for her daughter. She was so pleased to see her mother again and to catch up with all her news.

On her way back to the UK, she stopped off in Singapore, again to meet a South African businessman who had previously had a large restaurant in Beijing, but it had closed down because of his and his partner's inability to come to terms with how business negotiations were conducted in China. This meeting was very useful for her thesis because it gave the darker side of doing business in China.

Easter Holiday

I n May Lucy flew out to South Africa again, and this time she would be staying for a month. What a pleasure that was for Harry, to be together for so long. However, she was very busy whilst she was with him—lots of meetings to attend and lots of people to see. She had arranged interviews with the directors of some South African companies that had business interests in China, and she also arranged to attend a seminar at the Johannesburg Stock Exchange, which would be discussing Chinese-South African investments. She also met one of the diplomats in the commercial section of the Chinese embassy in Pretoria, as well as a retired senior South African diplomat who had previously been involved with South African business interests in China. It was a busy few weeks, but it was extremely useful for her PhD research. It was great for them as well to spend a lot of time together for a change. They did lots of things socially whilst she was here and had dinner with Des and Helene and a group of their friends at their house.

Whilst she was in South Africa, they talked about franchising Harry's business and selling franchises in other cities in South Africa—namely Johannesburg, Cape Town, Port Elizabeth, and Durban. Harry searched on the Internet and found that there was a company with offices not very far from his office in Pretoria, which specialised in selling franchises. He telephoned them and made an appointment to see whether they thought that it would be a worthwhile venture. Harry and Lucy duly went at the appointed time and met up with one of the directors of the company. He asked how long they had had the company and what the volume of their business was. Once they had told him all that he wanted to know, he said that he thought it would be a very good franchise to sell, and he wanted to include other cities and other countries as well. It all sounded very grand, but first they wanted to sell the franchises in South Africa before they even thought about any other countries. He said that he would draw up an agreement, and once his fee had been paid, he would start advertising the business. Harry and Lucy were very happy that they could do this. It had been a busy but productive month whilst Lucy had been in South Africa, but they also had urgent things to do in the UK as well, so on 10 June they flew back to the UK together.

UK—Visa Extension

When they arrived in London, they stayed in another guest house in Bloomsbury for a few days and had a lovely weekend, dining out and seeing another show before they got down to the business in hand on the Monday morning. Their first port of call was to Harry's old employers, to prepare Lucy's visa extension application. Her spouse/settlement visa, which had been issued in April 2009, was about to expire, and she had not been in the UK long enough for her to apply for her indefinite leave to remain, so they had to submit an application for her to extend her limited leave to remain visa. Thankfully it was prepared and submitted within a couple of days, and she received her extension of visa before they left London.

Whilst they were there in London, they had also arranged, through one of Harry's ex-colleagues (who had been working at the British embassy in Beijing when he was there on a leave relief in 1983), to meet up with someone in the Foreign and Commonwealth Office who was directly involved with British business interests in China. They duly went along to the FCO on Tuesday morning to attend the meeting. It felt quite strange for Harry to be going back into the FCO after so long away, but it brought back memories for him, some good and some bad. He was pleased to be away from all the bureaucratic nonsense, but there was still a sense of belonging. As it turned out, the meeting was not all that useful, and the guy they met did not seem to be fully aware of what doing business in China involved—he gave Lucy the party line on lots of the questions she asked him. Still, it was useful in some ways, and she was glad that they had actually managed to get in to see someone in the FCO. Lucy had even talked at one stage about joining the FCO once she got her British nationality, but knowing her as Harry did, he did not think that she would like it because from past experience, he knew that the wheels of bureaucracy often turn very slowly in the FCO, and Lucy liked things to happen quickly.

Once they had concluded all of their business in London, it was a case of taking the train up to Leeds because they were moving apartments. The apartment Lucy had been living in for the last eighteen months was beginning to get her down. Besides the noise of the traffic during the day, it seemed that every Friday evening and the early hours of Saturday morning, she was either serenaded by some drunks walking home along the pavement outside the apartment or woken up by police cars and ambulances using their sirens as they went roaring up and down the road. Friday night was party night in Leeds, and there was always a lot of noise outside of the apartment. They decided that it was time to move to somewhere quieter. They found a nice two-bedroom apartment in a quiet apartment block about half a mile away, which was still convenient for the bus station so that Lucy could get to the university and work; it was also convenient for walking into the centre of town for shopping. The move was quite time consuming because they could only fill their large suitcases and drag them along the pavement to the new place. It took most of the morning to move Lucy's stuff, but they eventually managed it and got everything sorted out in the new place. They decided that the second bedroom could be made into a study, so Harry dismantled the bed and put the mattress from that bed on top of the mattress in the main bedroom; it would make it more comfortable and would save them from having a mattress leaning against the wall in the study. He bought a desk and chair and some bookshelves, and by the time it was finished it looked really nice. Lucy was very happy to finally have a dedicated area where she could study instead of doing it all on the breakfast bar, as she had been doing in the old apartment. Once everything was sorted out, Harry flew back to South Africa a couple of days later.

Whilst they had been together, they had talked about starting a family. Lucy kept telling him about all the little ginger-haired boys and girls she had seen in Leeds, and because he used to have ginger hair when he was younger and had lived in Leeds, she kept teasing him saying that he must have been quite naughty when he was younger, if there were so many ginger-haired children wandering about. She said that she did not really want a little-ginger haired baby because her ideal child would have blonde hair and blue eyes—something which would be impossible given her Chinese origin. Harry would dearly have loved to have had a miniature Lucy; he had seen photographs of her when she was a baby and a toddler, and she looked so beautiful with a very mischievous smile and eyes. He felt sure that if they had ever had a little girl, she would have been exactly the same—as beautiful and as clever as her mother but also very mischievous as well. Lucy's Chinese name was Ling, and her mother used to call her Ling Ling when she was small. Harry kept wishing that they could have a little Ling Ling, but Lucy was not sure; she wanted to finish her studies first and get herself a good job before she started a family. She also felt that if they had a baby, she would no longer be Harry's little princess, and she did not want to relinquish this title just yet. They talked about it from time to time, but the answer was always the same: 'We will have one later.' She even said that she would freeze some of Harry's sperm so that if he proved incapable of making her pregnant by the normal method when he was older she could always use some of his sperm to have artificial insemination.

Business was going very well in South Africa, and it was September before Harry could find the time to visit Lucy in the UK again. They arranged to meet up in London as usual and decided that they would spend the whole of his visit in London. This time they would stay in a hotel rather than a guest house, especially because Harry's business was doing so well. They chose the Thistle Hotel in Marble Arch, which was very nice and conveniently located near the underground so that they could get around London to do what they wanted—shopping, dining out, and seeing some shows. It made a nice change from a guest house because it was much more comfortable, and the rooms were bigger. Harry was only able to be there for five days, so they had to squeeze as much as they could into the visit. They went to various markets and had lots of nice food in different restaurants, both in the centre of town and in Chelsea. It was on this visit that they first tried the Japanese restaurant in Harvey Nichols. It was really good, and they enjoyed it very much—so much so that they seemed to have piles of different coloured dishes, which indicated their price by their colour, stacked up on their table by the time they had finished eating. No wonder the chefs always recognised them each time they went back there on Harry's subsequent visits to the UK!

His next visit to see Lucy was in November. The main reason for this visit, besides wanting to see her again, was that the time had eventually arrived when she could apply for her indefinite leave to remain in the UK. It was vitally important that Harry be there so that they could prepare everything for submission. Harry had done quite a lot of the preparation in South Africa, but once he arrived in the UK, they decided that they should visit his old employer and colleagues in Sheffield so that they could submit the application on their behalf and get it processed quickly. They caught the train down to Sheffield on the Monday morning, and her application was submitted the following day. There was a small problem, however: when they had arrived in the UK together on 18 December 2009, the immigration officer at Leeds Bradford Airport—who they later found out had just completed his training—had not actually stamped the spouse visa in Lucy's passport but had stamped another page in the passport instead. By not stamping the visa, it had in effect not been activated, so when her application was submitted to the UK Border Agency, they said that she had applied too early and must wait another three or four months before making her application. Thankfully Harry's ex-colleague contacted them by phone and by letter, explaining what had happened. The matter was resolved a couple of days later, before Harry returned to South Africa. It was a worrying time for Lucy, and whilst they both knew that it would eventually be approved, it did not stop them worrying about it until they received her passport back along with her indefinite leave to remain card. What a relief, and she was now on the countdown for her British nationality and passport—only twelve months to go. Harry flew back to South Africa a happy man, relieved to know that everything was going according to plan.

Christmas in UK

H is next visit was for Christmas, and he left South Africa on 16 December and stayed until 1 January. It was the first time he had spent any length of time in their new apartment in Leeds, and it was wonderful. Lucy was still busy with her studies and work, but he simply enjoyed being with her, doing the shopping, and keeping the apartment tidy for when she got home. He was a real house husband. They had previously talked about Lucy flying out to South Africa so that they could spend Christmas in the sunshine, but she did not want to be out of the country in case it jeopardised her application for British nationality. It wouldn't have, really, because she was allowed to be out of the country for ninety days during that final twelve months, but Harry generally deferred to any request she made. Her happiness was very important to him.

They spent a quiet Christmas together and caught the train to see his friend Squire in Driffield so that they could have lunch together in the pub. They also met up with Harry's sister and her husband and his cousin and his wife for lunch, again in another pub. They had their Christmas lunch and dinner at home with lots of nice food that they had bought at Marks and Spencer.

During the time he was there, they also met up with some of Lucy's friends and colleagues from the university in a pub one evening. They all seemed very nice and had a fun evening chatting about different things, particularly Borneo, because a couple of the professors had been there doing some research of their own. Harry had been there numerous times before, and so they had a lot to talk about.

There were many good days over the Christmas period—days when they did nothing special aside from being together. It was a time of total contentment for Harry.

South Africa—Drive to Cape Town

He returned to South Africa at the beginning of January, and Lucy came out in March 2012. She had more people to see in Pretoria in connection with her research: people in Cape Town from the University of Cape Town, a businessman to meet in Stellenbosch, plus a meeting with a director of a wine company in the little town of Franshoek, about a forty minutes outside Cape Town. Following her meeting in Pretoria, they started the drive down to Cape Town on the Saturday; it was a long drive, some 1,457 miles. They left Pretoria at about 4.30 in the morning to try to get through Johannesburg before the morning traffic started, and they drove for thirteen hours before they reached the little town of Beaufort West, still some five hours' drive from Cape Town. They stopped off for the night at the Olive Grove guest house, which was situated inside an olive growing farm a few kilometres outside Beaufort West. It was a beautiful place nestled in the barren waste of the Karoo. The main house was some two or three kilometres from the main road, and there was a row of little single-storey townhouses where guests stayed. The inside of the little houses was basically just a bedroom with a toilet and shower, but they were very comfortable, and it was peaceful there after the long drive. They were made very welcome by the owners and did not have long to wait after they arrived before dinner was served in the main house. It was good home cooking, and shortly after dinner they retired to their little house to catch up on some sleep before the next leg of the journey. Before they left, they booked a room for their return journey, and much to their amazement the lady in the reception said that she wouldn't give them a bill for this visit but would lump it all together when they stayed there on their way back to Pretoria. She was very trusting.

Next morning after a really good breakfast, they were on their way again to Cape Town, but they did not drive straight there. They stopped off at the Cango Caves some twenty-nine kilometres from Oudtshoorn and went underground. The caves were enormous, approximately one thousand metres in length with the largest chamber being three hundred metres in length. The guides said that a hundred jumbo jets could be parked in this chamber. Harry had been there previously when he'd lived in South Africa between 1986 and 1989, but this was Lucy's first visit. There were some amazing rock formations inside the caves with stalactites, stalagmites, and also organ pipes, where the stalactites and stalagmites joined together.

As soon as they surfaced, they continued their drive to Cape Town along the scenic route, which involved a lot of twisting roads, some of which ran through the bottom of various gorges with mountains towering above them on either side. They eventually reached Cape Town in the middle of the afternoon after driving for a total of eighteen hours. It had been a long drive but one that Harry had enjoyed. It was nice to drive long distances when he was in a nice car with a beautiful girl for company, as well as nice weather and not much traffic on the road. The journey did not feel as long as it was because he had Lucy at his side.

Upon arrival in Cape Town, they checked into the Breakwater Hotel, which was near the waterfront and had been converted from its original use as a prison. It was attached to the Cape Town University Business School, where Lucy had arranged to meet with one of the academics. They stayed in Cape Town for a couple of days and spent a lot of time in the waterfront wandering about and having nice meals. On Wednesday they drove up to Stellenbosch so that Lucy could meet with the director of an information technology company that had business interests in China. The meeting went very well, and they then drove to Franshoek for her next meeting at the Leopards Leap Winery. Whilst she was in her meeting, Harry was able to wander around the office and look at all the wines and the kitchen implements they had on display. The meeting went well, and she gained a lot of very useful information to include in her research. Once her meeting was over, they were offered a wine-tasting session, which resulted in them buying some wine to take home with them.

As soon as Lucy's meeting in the Cape concluded, they started their return journey to Pretoria, stopping off again at the Olive Grove Guest house in Beaufort West, where they arrived just in time for dinner. Next morning they left before breakfast was served so that they could get on the road and start the thirteen-hour drive back to Pretoria. On their way down to Cape Town, there had been lots and lots of road works that caused them some considerable delays, so Harry decided, rather than drive up the N1 road, that he would take an alternative route and drive across the Karoo via Kimberley. It was a much easier drive, and even though there were a few road works, they did not get delayed as much this way as they had on the way down, which meant that they arrived back in Pretoria at a reasonable time, tired but relieved to be home again. Harry was working the next day, so Lucy was able to stay in bed late and then start making notes from her various meetings.

That evening they were invited to Des and Helene's for dinner, but it was Lucy who was preparing the dinner—eleven Chinese dishes in all. Luckily she had help with the preparation; Helene and her two maids assisted with the cleaning and chopping of vegetables, so it made Lucy's job a lot easier—just the cooking to do later in the evening. The dinner went off really well, and everyone said what fantastic food it was; they had never tasted such delicious Chinese food before. Lucy was pleased, and Harry was so proud of her, as always. One of the guests present, who had some strong business interests with China, invited Lucy to visit his company, which manufactured pylons and other things made out of steel.

The day before she was supposed to go to the steel company, Lucy had to attend a seminar at the Johannesburg stock exchange. Harry drove her through after he finished work, and he sat outside until the seminar was over. As usual she was one of the last to emerge from the meeting room because she had been chatting with all the people who had been on the panel to find out as much as possible about what they were doing.

The visit to the steel company the following day was a bit of a rush. Lucy had to be there at a certain time, and Harry had clients booked for the same time. They managed to get her there in time, and then he had to race back to his office to meet clients. He was surprised that he did not get a speeding fine considering how fast he had to drive. Once he had finished with them a couple of hours later, he went back to collect her. She said that it had been a very good meeting and that she had learned a lot. She returned to the UK on 8 April to continue with her studies and also to continue working for her employers.

In July 2012 Harry sold his first franchise office in South Africa, in Johannesburg. He sold it at a knock-down price because it was the first one. Once the sale was completed and all the fees had been paid, he spent a few days training the man who had bought it, Brian, and he opened the office at the beginning of August. It proved to be a very successful and lucrative business for him almost from the day he opened his office. Brian had managed to secure an office in the same office block as the centre where people submitted their visa applications and was extremely busy from day one; he recouped his investment within about three months of opening. Harry did not mind because Brian was a very good businessman and was quick to learn; he also had some good ideas that would improve the business and make the company more prominent in the field of visas, and not only for the UK.

Within a short period of time of Brian opening, he started talking about buying the Pretoria office from Harry for his wife to run. Harry was pleased at the interest in taking over another office, but he still wanted to sell other franchises first.

Flying visit to UK— Wedding Anniversary

Shortly after he had completed the training with Brian for the Johannesburg office, he flew back to the UK for a quick visit so that he could be with Lucy on their fourth wedding anniversary. It was a very quick visit—he arrived on Friday 13 and left on Monday 16—but it was worth it to be with Lucy on this special day, to take her out for dinner, and buy her a nice anniversary present. They had an expensive dinner in the Windows Restaurant in the Park Lane Hilton Hotel. The restaurant was on the top floor of the hotel, and as the name suggests it had windows all around. From their table they could see the Buckingham Palace gardens out of the window, and it was a perfect setting for their anniversary dinner. They wondered if they might see the Queen and the Duke of Edinburgh having a wander around the gardens, but they didn't. It really was a special anniversary dinner, and the food and service was outstanding. Harry loved being with her in these kinds of surroundings; she always looked so comfortable and caused a lot of heads to turn. He was so much in love with her and felt like the luckiest man alive.

Over the weekend they went out shopping during the day and had dinner before they went to watch a show in the evening. He loved being with Lucy no matter where they were. On Monday, the day he was flying back to South Africa, they went shopping to buy Lucy a desktop Apple computer because the one she had been using was a little bit small, and she needed something bigger for her research. They went along to PC World in Regent Street and found the latest model, which was very nice indeed and was very sleek looking. It was a little bit expensive, but if it was going to make Lucy's life and research easier, it was worth it. When the shop assistant brought out the new computer all packed in its box, Harry was wondering, given the size of the box, how on earth Lucy would get it back to Leeds, especially because she already had some luggage. They took a taxi back to the hotel to collect the rest of their luggage and then took another taxi to the railway station, where they commandeered a trolley and wheeled Lucy's luggage to the train. Once she and all her luggage were on board, they had their final hug and kiss before the train departed. Harry hated saying goodbye to her, and he was also worried how she would manage with all her baggage once she got to Leeds. He waited on the platform to see the train pull out and walked alongside the train blowing kisses at her and waving until the train picked up speed and he was no longer able to keep up. She looked so beautiful and happy after their weekend together.

His concerns about how she would manage to carry all her belongings once she reached Leeds were unfounded. She told him later that she received some assistance from a kind man when she was getting off the train; he helped her load all her belongings onto a trolley, which she wheeled to the taxi rank, and she caught a taxi to take her home. She was absolutely delighted with the computer once she had set it all up, and it proved to be a very useful purchase. Harry was so happy for her—anything which made her life easier was all right by him.

Flying visit to UK— Lucy's 30th Birthday

A month later, in August, Harry flew back to the UK again, this time for her thirtieth birthday—another special date which he wanted to spend with her. A thirtieth birthday for some ladies was often a day when they start thinking that they were no longer young girls and had now reached womanhood, so he wanted to be with her on this date. It was another quick visit; he arrived on her birthday, 16 August; they met in London; and he returned to South Africa on 19 August. They stayed at the Thistle Hotel in Marble Arch again, and during the afternoon they went shopping.

Harry asked Lucy what present she would like for her birthday, and she said she dared not tell him. Eventually after much persuasion she did: what she really wanted most of all was a Chanel bag. Harry suggested that they go and look for one. When they arrived in the little Chanel shop on Old Bond Street, they immediately started looking at all different sorts of bags until Lucy found one she really liked. Harry did not know how expensive they were until it came time to pay, but it did not matter—it was for his little princess, and she could have anything she wanted. Lucy was over the moon with the bag and said that her colleagues in her office would be jealous of it when she went back to Leeds. During this short visit they managed to squeeze in quite a lot. They went out for dinner every evening and had a glorious time together during the day, because she had taken time off work and from her studies. Whilst in London they took the train to visit King Henry VIII palace at Hampton Court or as Lucy called it Henry's House which is situated in the London Borough of Richmond upon Thames—about 12 miles outside of central London. The palace was originally built for Cardinal Thomas Wolsey in the 16th Century, but once he fell from the King's favour the palace was taken over by the King who enlarged it to what it is today. It was a wonderful day—the weather was perfect and the palace and the gardens were really spectacular and they both enjoyed their first ever visit to this historical site. Harry loved being with her every minute of the day and night. She was such a lovely person to be with, and they used to have so much fun and laughter when they were together. He hated leaving her when it was time to return to South Africa.

Move to Shanghai?

Lucy had been working for the company in Leeds for more than two years by this time and was beginning to be heavily involved with all of their projects in China, so much so that they started talking about opening an office in Shanghai— and they wanted her to go there to be their business manager for the whole of China. She was very excited about this, although at the same time she a little bit apprehensive at the responsibility she was going to be given. Harry told her that she would be fine and that he had every confidence in her ability to do this job. She said that she would like to finish off her PhD before she left so that there would be one less thing to worry about.

Her workload in the office started to increase, and she was working more and more days each week—sometimes as many as four days per week. She was also taking work home with her to do in the evening. All this was on top of her PhD research. She was working so hard, sometimes seventeen hours per day, and the strain was beginning to tell. Her PhD research started suffering because she was spending so much time on the office work. Her supervisor from the university kept sending her mails asking her to meet him and also to submit some of her work to him. It was becoming quite stressful for her, but somehow she managed to cope with it all.

They were talking about when she would be going to Shanghai and how they would work it all out. She said that it would probably be around June 2013 before she would go, and she stated that she would like to go on her own initially because she would be very busy setting everything up as well as having meetings with lots of Chinese companies. Harry was happy with this because he still wanted to sell more of the franchises so that they could have a steady income from royalties once he left South Africa.

In September Brian from the Johannesburg office started talking seriously about buying the Pretoria office for his wife, and he mentioned that he was interested in buying the Cape Town franchise for his son. There was also interest in the Port Elizabeth franchise. Things were looking up, and Harry was quite excited because everything seemed be going according to plan, which meant that he would probably be able to leave South Africa in June or July and go to Shanghai not long after Lucy arrived.

He flew back to the UK again in the middle of September mainly because he wanted to see Lucy so that they could talk about their plans for going to China, and also because the following Monday was a public holiday in South Africa, so he could make it into a long weekend. He arrived on Thursday and flew back on Monday. Whilst he was in the UK, they talked a lot about their plans for the future and how they would work out all the logistics of relocating to Shanghai. She would take some things from their apartment in the UK, and he would take some things from South Africa. They also talked about buying the apartment they were renting so that they would have somewhere which they could call home, and also somewhere they would be able to leave all of the belongings which they would not need in Shanghai.

Lucy was very focused on the job in China and wanted to make sure that she was successful once she got there. Harry suggested what kinds of things she should expect the company to provide for her—such as paying for her flight, his flight, hotel expenses upon arrival, shipping expenses for all of her clothes and shoes that would not fit into her normal baggage allowance, an accommodation allowance, medical insurance, and flights to and from the UK during holidays. She seemed a little bit uncertain about asking for so many things and said that although she knew that when he worked for the Foreign Office they had paid for all of these kinds of expenses, but she was not sure whether a commercial company would do the same. He tried to reassure her that normally commercial companies provided their staff with better benefits than the government. She was still not entirely sure, but at least he felt better from suggesting what she should expect.

Franchise Sales

When he arrived back in South Africa, things started moving quickly with the sale of the Pretoria office, and there was also very strong interest from the man who wanted to buy the Port Elizabeth franchise. Brian's wife took over the Pretoria office at the beginning of November, and Harry started making plans to move to Cape Town to open an office there. Before he left for Cape Town, he was told that there was someone who wanted to buy the Cape Town franchise even before it was opened. Negotiations on the Port Elizabeth office were also moving quite quickly; the businessman who was interested in buying it had paid his deposit and was waiting for Harry to arrange when he could start the training programme for the lady who was going to run the office for him, before he paid the balance. It was a hectic time.

Harry flew down to Cape Town to try to find an office space in the same office block as where the UK visa collection centre was located. The person he met from the management company who managed that building told him that there were no office spaces available in that building, but there was a small office in the building next door. Harry was not very happy with this, but the office that he saw seemed to have potential and was not too far away from the visa collection centre, so he decided he would have to accept that this was as close as he was going to get for the time being. He also found a nice apartment in Sea Point that had two bedrooms, a kitchen, and a lounge and dining area. The main bedroom was what really attracted him because it had a bathroom en-suite. At first he thought there must be a glass wall between the bedroom and the bathroom, but there wasn't—the bathroom was part of the bedroom. It was so unusual that he decided to take it. The view from the apartment was another deciding factor: from the lounge and main bedroom windows, he could see Table Mountain, Lions Head, and also the sea—fantastic views.

Move to Cape Town

He returned to Pretoria a couple of days later to start arranging his move to Cape Town and also to arrange a convenient time when he could do the training in Port Elizabeth. He contacted an auctioneer company to come and collect all of his furniture so that it could be sold at auction, and once the apartment was empty and cleaned up, he loaded his car and drove down to Cape Town on 29 November, stopping overnight at the Olive Grove guest house in Beaufort West. He arrived in Cape Town on 30 November and moved into his new, fully furnished apartment. On 3 December he flew to Port Elizabeth to start a week's training course with the lady who would be running the franchise. He returned to Cape Town next Friday evening.

The Cape Town office was a bit of a shambles when he moved in; the walls were filthy and so were the carpets. There was also a lot of furniture that had been left in there by the previous tenant, so it was not really fit for purpose. He had been assured by the management company, which was the same company that managed the ABSA centre where the visa collection centre was located, that everything would be done before he moved in—walls painted and carpets cleaned. It wasn't. It took days of continuous nagging on his part before the painter eventually arrived on 13 December and started to paint the walls of the office. He finished the next day, and Harry flew to the UK for Christmas that evening. There was still a bit to do in the office before he could get his office furniture installed and start receiving clients.

Last Christmas in UK

He arrived in London on 15 December and arranged to meet Lucy in London so that they could go to a show on 16 December. It was a performance by a South African singing group called Romanz which consisted of four young men whom Harry had helped with their visas a couple of months earlier, so that they could travel to the UK to promote themselves. Harry had become quite friendly with them during the course of their visa applications, and they had arranged that he and Lucy would be given complimentary tickets to their show in London. They stayed at the Hilton Metropole Hotel this time, and the show was in Leicester Square in a casino. The performance was really good, and it was great to see the members of the group again and to introduce Lucy to them. They told her that they recognised her immediately from all the photographs they had seen on Harry's desk in his office in Pretoria. It was a lovely evening, and they had dinner afterwards in a nice little steak restaurant close to the casino.

The following morning they went to see Harry's old employer to hand over all the documents for Lucy's British nationality application. They had agreed to do it for them free of charge, apart from the Home Office fee, because Harry was referring some of his South African clients to them who needed to have their visas extended once they were in the UK. Marie, the director, who always played things down, told them that it would take two or three months before they heard anything, and it could be as long as six months before Lucy got her passport. They were a little bit worried if it was going to take six months, but even if it did, it should be all done by the time Lucy had to leave for Shanghai. Still, they knew how much Marie always exaggerated, so they were not overly concerned.

They took the train up to Leeds that afternoon and started to prepare for what would be their last Christmas in the UK for some time. Whilst Harry had been in the UK on his last visit, he had ordered a goose from a butcher's shop in the market for them to collect before Christmas, so that they could have it for their lunch on Christmas Day. It was the first time that either of them had tried goose, but they thought it would make a change from turkey. They bought all the rest of the Christmas fare at Marks and Spencer and were ready for Christmas Day to come. They did the usual last-minute Christmas shopping and sent Christmas cards to family and friends in the hope that they would be delivered before Christmas Day. Harry went over to see his sister one day before Christmas whilst Lucy was working, and then it was a matter of waiting for Christmas Day to arrive.

It was during his Christmas visit that Lucy and Harry went to see her dentist. She had been seeing him pretty regularly on a private fee basis because a lot of the dental work that she had had done in China was not of a very high standard, and some of her crowns kept falling out. The dentist had told her that what she really needed was to have all of her teeth replaced with porcelain teeth, and then she would have no more trouble for several years. They had discussed this previously and decided that even though it was going to be very expensive, because she was one of his private patients it would be worth doing, especially before she returned to China in June 2013. The dentist said that she would need four or five appointments over a period of about two months before he could finish all the work, so the quicker he started, the quicker it would be finished. Harry had transferred GBP19,000 into Lucy's bank account before he left South Africa, and she gave the dentist a cheque whilst they were there. He said that he would start the work in the New Year. They were both pleased that finally she would have all her dental work done properly and would not have any more discomfort in the future with her teeth.

They had a wonderful Christmas together, but they were not so enamoured with the goose; there was very little meat on it, but they had enough goose fat left over to cook plenty of roast potatoes for months to come. Still, the main thing was that they were together for Christmas.

Back to South Africa

Harry returned to South Africa on 3 January, and Lucy resumed her work and her studies in earnest. She was very busy, working long hours in the office and then getting home in the evening to do her university work. The strain was beginning to take its toll; she was very tired and started to feel stressed about everything she had to do before she left for Shanghai. Work in her office was becoming more and more demanding, so much so that she was leaving for the office at 7.00 AM in the mornings and not getting home until sometimes as late as 9.00 or 10.00 PM and then doing some of her university work. They were still speaking to each other five times per day and exchanging e-mails, but Harry could tell that she was tired, and he worried about her physical and mental health.

When he arrived back in Cape Town, the office was still not as he wanted it—the carpets had not been cleaned and the old furniture was still in situ. He could not start seeing clients with it like this, and it was becoming quite frustrating. Eventually the carpets were cleaned and the furniture was removed, but by this time it was halfway through the month. He had some new office furniture delivered, and the office started to look something like he wanted it. But it was the last week in January before he started receiving any clients, which meant that he had effectively lost almost two months business since he'd moved down.

Shortly after he got back, Lucy phoned Harry to say that she had been invited to attend the passport interview, where they checked that the person applying for the passport was the same person who signed the passport application form. This turnaround was much quicker than they or Marie had expected; it came about because someone had cancelled their existing appointment. They were both delighted and excited that it was going to take place so soon. A couple of weeks later Lucy attended the interview, which was just as they had expected it would be; it lasted about twenty minutes. It was now simply a case of waiting for the date the actual ceremony, when she would receive her certificate of naturalisation.

Things really took off regarding her move to Shanghai. Lucy had already been to China in February on a familiarisation trip and to give a presentation to a large international client in Shanghai, which resulted in her company being awarded a very lucrative contract. Now it was getting closer to her move, and there was still a lot to be done. She had various training courses to attend in her office whilst still working full time and also finishing her studies. She planned to hand in everything but the concluding chapter of her PhD thesis to her supervisor before she left in June.

A few days after Harry's office became fully functioinal, he received a phone call from a different leasing company asking him if he was interested in having an office in the ABSA centre—the same office building where the visa collection centre was situated. He was surprised and said that he did not think there were any offices available in that building. The agent told him that there were quite a few vacant offices. Harry immediately contacted the management company who had leased him his existing office and asked them if there were offices available. The girl he spoke to said there was, so he asked her if he could go and have a look at them.

As they were walking over to the office, she told him which floors the empty offices were on, and then she dropped the biggest bombshell. She told him that there was an empty office on the same floor as the visa collection centre—exactly where he wanted to be. When he asked her when the office had become available, she told him that it was in November 2012. The tenants who were already renting two other higher floors in the building had decided to move their reception area from the twenty-second floor to the same floor as their main office. Harry was flabbergasted and said that if they'd moved in November, then they must have given notice to the management company in September or October—before he came down to Cape Town to look for office space. It appeared that he had been misled by the salesperson who had told him that there were no offices in that building. He felt annoyed and immediately started making inquiries, which were all denied. He resolved to get that office in the ABSA centre and was told that if he found a tenant to take over his existing office, then they would agree to let him move to the ABSA centre. It took some time, but eventually a solution was reached. Still, it took a few months before he was allowed to move.

British Nationality

I n March Harry flew back to the UK for Easter and also to attend Lucy's British nationality ceremony, when she would have to swear an oath of allegiance to the Queen; the ceremony was being held in the Leeds town hall. Lucy was very excited about this and was a little bit nervous in case she forgot what to say. He told her that there would be a little card from which she could read, and that she should not worry because he was sure that she would be fine.

A couple of weeks before Harry arrived in the UK, Lucy had been telling him how stressed she was and how she needed something to cheer herself up. She told him that she had been looking at a sapphire necklace which matched the sapphire bracelet he had bought her a few months earlier. She said that she kept going into Harvey Nichols to look at it each time she felt depressed. He told her to go and buy it, if it would make her feel happy; her happiness was very important to him. She phoned him the next day to say that she had bought it and was feeling much better. She really liked it and said that it would make all of her colleagues in the office even more envious of her. They already thought that she lived on a different planet to them because she lived in a nice apartment, had a cleaning company who did the cleaning, and had a husband who bought her a Chanel bag and earrings and some Gucci boots, as well as lots of other designer items. They laughed together, and he was so pleased for her and told her how beautiful she would look wearing the new necklace in the office.

A couple of days later, she sent him an e-mail saying that she was starting to worry about him going to Shanghai with her when she went. She said that she was going to be extremely busy initially and did not want to be worrying about him sitting at home all alone whilst she was away on business trips. He tried to reassure her that he would not be joining her until after she had settled in, and once he arrived in Shanghai he would continue to do the English language marking, which he was already doing in South Africa. He knew from one of his friends in Beijing who was doing this English language marking for the British Council that it was almost a full-time job; he would be visiting different cities each weekend to do the speaking tests, and then for the following three days he would be marking the writing tests. His friend had told Harry that he was really busy in Beijing, and Harry expected Shanghai to be the same because there were three hundred thousand people in China taking these tests each year—which was a lot of marking. Harry estimated that they could live on what he would earn from the English marking, and she would be able to bank all of her salary in the UK. He asked if she had spoken to anyone in her office about whether they would be paying his airfare to fly out to join her in Shanghai once she had got the office up and running. She said she hadn't because she was not sure that they would pay. He found this to be a bit surprising, especially given that they were married and her company were sending her there to open their office. Surely they would not object to paying her husband's fare as well.

He arrived back in the UK on the Monday, and Lucy's nationality ceremony was held on the Thursday of that week. They arrived at the town hall quite early, as they usually did for any appointment, and had to wait while all the other recipients arrived. The ceremony, which was presided over by the Lord Lieutenant of Leeds, acting on behalf of the Queen, eventually got underway. The Lord Lieutenant looked very splendid in his army dress uniform with his sword hanging at his side. After a welcoming speech by one of the officials from the town hall, each person was invited to go up to the front and swear the oath of allegiance and then shake hands with the Lord Lieutenant. A photographer was on hand to capture this moment, and if friends or relatives of the recipient wanted to have their photograph taken, then they could go up, and the photographer would take a second photograph. Lucy had her photograph taken with the Lord Lieutenant while holding her certificate, but Harry declined the offer to be included in a second photo, saying that it was Lucy's day and not his.

As soon as the ceremony was over, they went to celebrate in one of their favourite restaurants, Brown's, on the Headrow in Leeds; it was almost next door to the town hall. They went in and ordered champagne and fish and chips with mushy peas—similar to what they'd had on their first outing to the Dales in 2006, except with champagne this time instead of a pot of tea. Harry had collected a passport application form from the post office the previous day, and Lucy had already had it countersigned by someone in her office, so as soon as they sat down waiting for their lunch, they started to complete the rest of her passport application form; Harry filled it in and Lucy signed it. Immediately after lunch, he took it straight to the post office only to be told that Lucy's signature had gone slightly over the edge of the box where she had to sign and that it would not be acceptable. He had to get another form and redo it, and Lucy also had to get it signed by a witness. Thankfully all this was done in time for him to take it back to the post office the following day, which was the day before he had to return to South Africa.

Before he left, they went to Lucy's bank to speak to one of the managers about getting a mortgage so that they could buy a property in the UK, likely the apartment they were renting, so that they would have somewhere to leave all of their stuff and have somewhere they could call home. The bank said that with Lucy's substantial new salary, they could easily give her a good mortgage, but unfortunately they would not include Harry's income into the account because he worked overseas. They decided that Harry would pay the deposit on the apartment and that Lucy would have the mortgage in her name. They felt quite pleased that eventually they would have a place they could call their and that with Lucy's income, which was going to be quite significant, the bank was happy to give her a good mortgage.

Lucy received her British passport at the beginning of April. She was delighted, and so was Harry. It had taken some time, but she was now British and would be able to travel to lots of countries in the future without the need to apply for a visa first. But going to China on a British passport still required one. She joked that nothing had really changed; she always had to apply for a visa anywhere she had been previously using her Chinese passport, and she was still having to do the same again now with her British passport.

Devastated

Harry had always believed that Lucy was an honest, reliable, self-assured, and determined young lady, and he trusted her completely, but he was unable to predict the course of action she would take that would lead to the total destruction of his life. Although the warning signs were there, he was so much in love with Lucy that he had not seen them, or if he had, he had not read them.

A few days after she had received her British passport, the bottom dropped out of his world. She sent him an e-mail saying that she did not want him to join her in Shanghai after all, and she would prefer to be there on her own, even though it meant that she could be there for up to five years. He was devastated and asked her what the reason was behind this decision, especially because they had been making plans for so long to be there together. She said that she would be worrying about him if he went with her, and they should talk about it face to face when he was next in the UK at the end of May, to pack up the apartment. He was racking his brain and trying to think about what had brought about this decision. He thought perhaps she was remembering the Chinese guy in the Japanese restaurant who had assumed that Lucy was a prostitute because she was with an older man. He simply could not understand why she had suddenly reached this decision, and he was unable to sleep properly at nights, but he lived in the hope that they would be able to resolve the problem when they next spoke face to face.

Before he returned to the UK, he thought it would be a good idea to book a hotel for the week he was going to be there so that they would have somewhere to stay whilst they packed up the apartment. He asked Lucy if she wanted him to include breakfast for her, and whether she would have time to eat it before she left for the office. She said that she would not be staying in the hotel with him because she would move out of the apartment before he arrived and would stay with a friend. She said that he could stay in the apartment on his own if he liked, rather than in the hotel. This conversation made him even more depressed.

Besides worrying about Lucy and their future together, Harry was also very concerned about what was happening in South Africa. Talk about Lucy having stress—he had plenty of his own. The landlord of his apartment had telephoned him the week before saying that he had found a new tenant to take over the apartment who was going to pay him 10 per cent more than Harry was, and he had accepted the tenancy because it was a corporate let for twelve months. Harry said that he had been hoping to stay there and extend his six-month contract, but the landlord said that he couldn't do this now and that Harry must move out before the end of the month. What a disaster. Harry quickly found a new apartment in Green Point and arranged to move in a two days before he left for the UK. The move over the two days was hectic, loading the car up, then emptying it at the new apartment, and then putting everything away before returning to the old apartment to give it a final clean.

On top of this, the new office in the ABSA centre also required his attention before he left. He had to arrange for someone to go in there and build dry walls to create separate offices inside, and also to have the place painted and decorated. It was a lot of pressure, but thankfully everything came together.

When he arrived in Leeds at the end of May, he checked into the hotel and went to the apartment to meet Lucy. They arrived almost at the same time, and she looked very tired and very serious. They decided that rather than sit in the apartment, which was pretty bare by that time because she had already moved all of her stuff out, they would go to the hotel and sit in the quiet bar at the back of the reception area. When they got there, they ordered coffee and then started to talk about why she had reached her decision. He asked her to be brutally honest with him and tell him what was going on, even if she told him that she had found someone else. She said she had not found someone else, but she had been thinking about it since before Christmas. She had not told him then because she thought it would have spoiled their Christmas together. He then asked her why she had not told him in March when he was in the UK, and again she said she did not want to cause him any pain whilst he was with her. She simply felt now that she wanted to be on her own. She acknowledged that he had taken care of her, supported her, and protected her all of the time that they had been together, and she knew that he loved her more than anybody in the world, but she wanted to start her new life on her own.

He said that it did look like a bit of a coincidence that she had been thinking about leaving him around the same time that she had submitted her British nationality application and that once she got her British nationality, had a good job with a really good salary, and had her teeth fixed that she did not need him anymore. She said that this was hurtful and that it had not been her intention. She simply felt that she needed to be on her own to prove to herself that she could survive without him. She repeated the fact that she would be travelling a lot with her job and did not want to worry about him sitting at home alone whilst she was gone. She also said that she had realised that by the time she was fifty years old, she would probably be on her own because Harry would most likely have died by that time. Although he could understand her reasoning on this, he reminded her that shortly after they first met, he had told her that he was too old for her and that she had said then that the age difference did not matter. She went on to say that even though she thought she was mature at that time and that the decision had seemed right then, it did not seem right anymore. As much as he could see her point of view, it still seemed cruel, considering he had built his life around her and given her everything she wanted. He asked her why they had bothered going to the bank to ask about a mortgage, and again she said that she thought it would make him happy to think that they were going to have a home together.

She was quite tearful at times, but they managed to keep the conversation cordial without either of them over-reacting. She said that she knew that she would be punished later in life for what she was doing to him, but she was prepared to accept this. She told him that she had been living with a girl, who was a post-doctoral student at the university, for the past few weeks, and she said that he should move into the apartment instead of paying a few hundred pounds for the hotel. Harry responded by saying that he could not possibly live there on his own—there were too many memories for him there.

They parted company after an hour with a promise that they would meet again later in the week. She gave him the keys to the apartment so that he could go in, clean the place, and reassemble the bed in the second bedroom.

He went to the apartment shortly after she had left the hotel and found the place to be completely empty apart from the study/bedroom, which still had all the furniture and lots of his books in there; some of his clothes which he had left in the UK were also hanging in the wardrobe. All traces of Lucy ever having been there had been removed. On the desk in the study he found her wedding and engagement rings, his will, and the credit card she had been using on his account. It was an awful feeling. He had been hoping that she might change her mind, but it seemed she would not. This really brought it home to him that she was leaving for good.

The next morning he went so see a divorce lawyer in Leeds, and he told Harry that because he was not domicile in the UK, he could not apply for a divorce in the UK. He called Lucy to tell her what the lawyer had said, and she was not happy; she said that she would speak to someone in the legal department of her company. It was almost as though she wanted Harry out of her hair as quickly as possible. She called him back later to say that she had been advised by one of the company lawyers that they should be able to apply for a divorce and that they should meet at the Crown Courts in Leeds the following morning so that they could go in to collect a divorce pack, which they could complete together and return it to the courts as soon as it was done. They met the following morning quite early and collected the divorce papers, which they completed, one copy for each of them. Lucy took them to hand in the following morning and paid for the fees.

They met up a few times whilst he was there. On Wednesday they met in the apartment to start packing up all the things which they were going to leave in storage. The cardboard boxes had been delivered previously, and Lucy had also arranged to rent a storage locker. They sat talking together in the apartment as though nothing had happened, waiting for the removal men to arrive. When the men did arrive, it seemed as though they were expecting just to collect their belongings and not pack them, so Harry and Lucy had to start packing lots of books and other items whilst the removal men took some of the furniture to their van. It was fun working together again, and they had quite a few laughs whilst they were doing it—just like old times. It was sad in a way that they could still be happy together but were separating for good. They walked to the storage depot together, even holding hands as they crossed the roads. Once there Lucy completed all the forms and told Harry what the combination of the padlock on the door of the storage locker would be so that he could gain access to it should he need to recover his belongings at some stage.

They met in Browns and had lunch together on Thursday. She said that she would pay for his hotel, but Harry told her that it had been paid in advance. They were still friends, but the magic had certainly gone as far as she was concerned. She said that she loved him in her own way, but it did not feel like it had before. Something else she said which was quite interesting. She said that none of his family—neither his sister nor his cousins—had ever contacted her whilst she had been on her own in Leeds, not even to phone to ask how she was or to invite her to their homes for a cup of tea or a meal. It seemed to her that she was in exactly the same position as she and mother had been with her father's family: part of nothing and not wanted. Harry tried to tell her that his sister and her husband were both busy and that they hardly ever contacted *him* whilst he was overseas, and he added that he did not see anyone in the UK apart from her. She was his family, and all that he cared about—he didn't need anyone else. But he could tell that this was falling on deaf ears; she had made her decision and was sticking to it—there was no turning back.

On Friday, the day before he was leaving, he asked her if they could have one last dinner together. She said that she was going out with her colleagues from the office that evening, but they could meet up for lunch in Browns, and they did. She arrived carrying a large box that contained a new laptop computer which she had been given by her company. He asked her why she had brought it to the lunch, if she was going back to the office in the afternoon and going out with her colleagues that evening. She said she was not going back to the office but was going to her friend's house to finish her packing. He had no idea what she was doing or even where she was going. As much as he doubted what she told him, there was no point in pressing her for details because it would not make any difference to their current situation. They had lunch together, and she then gave him a cheque for GBP1,000 and said that it was to help to pay for the hotel and for his airfare. He was reluctant to accept it but thought, *What the hell, I may as well.* His bank account was not so healthy any more after paying for her teeth and the sapphire necklace, as well as his flight and the hotel.

She told him that she was flying British Airways from London, not KLM from Leeds as she had done on her previous trip to Shanghai earlier in the year. He found this quite strange and could not understand why the company would go to the expense of paying for her train fare and her overnight hotel accommodation in London, when she could easily have flown from Leeds by KLM. He was flying KLM from Leeds, which made him think that there was more to her reasons for flying from London than she was letting on. She said the reason for going via London was that she could travel business class with British Airways, because the fare was cheaper and would give her more luggage allowance. It seemed a pretty weak excuse, but there was no point in pressing her, even though he tried. She did not want him to know what she was doing anymore.

They left the restaurant together and stood outside to say their goodbyes—one last hug and one last kiss. He told her that he still loved her and would always love her, and then he turned around and walked away without looking back, even though he wanted to. The only true love his life had always been and would always remain Lucy, but their marriage was over. He was heartbroken and left for South Africa the following morning.

Shortly after he arrived back in South Africa, she sent him a mail saying that she had arrived safely in Shanghai and that she had spoken to one of her PhD colleagues who was from Vietnam. He had said that he would try to help Harry, if he ever decided to go there to open up a business in the future. A couple of days later, he sent her a mail asking if she had found an apartment to live in, or whether she was still in a hotel. She did not reply. He waited a couple of days and then sent an e-mail to her PhD supervisor to ask him if he had heard from her and whether she had handed in the work before she left, as she told him she would. He replied almost immediately, saying how pleased he was that he had contacted him because he was worried about Lucy—she had not given him any of her work since before Christmas, which made Harry wonder even more what she had been doing since then. Her supervisor then sent her an e-mail saying that Harry had contacted him and was concerned about her.

Within a matter of minutes she sent Harry a very angry e-mail telling him to leave her alone and to stop interfering in her life. He was totally shocked and replied that he had been worried about her. He asked why she had lied to him about submitting the work to her supervisor. Shortly afterwards he received another e-mail from her supervisor saying that Lucy had just sent him a heap of writing, which he would be looking at as soon as he had the time.

A little while later Lucy telephoned him from Shanghai. She was still quite angry with him for contacting her supervisor, but at least during their conversation he found out more about her reasons for leaving him. She told him that she felt as though she had been a prisoner for the last eight years, especially over the last three years because she had had to rush home in the evening if she had been out with friends to send him an e-mail to let him know what she had been doing during the day and to let him know she was all right. He tried to explain that it was only natural for him to worry when he knew that she would be walking home in the dark, and he simply wanted to know that she was safe. She then said that she had given him her youth, and that it was time she was on her own. He reminded her that he had told her just after they had met that he was too old for her and that he would be depriving her of her youth, but she was not really listening. He also told her that she had had a free hand for the last three and a half years, and she had more friends in the UK than he did in South Africa—the only friends he had in South Africa were Des and Helene. He was going to work each day and going home in the afternoon without seeing anyone apart from clients. He was living like a hermit and was not going out, just to provide for her.

She was still not listening and went on to say that he was not a proper man because he had not given her a family or a home. Now they were getting down to the real reasons why she decided that she wanted to be on her own. He reminded her that she always insisted on him wearing a condom when they made love, and that in any case she had always said—and had even told their friends in South Africa—that she did not want a family. He had been happy to respect her decision because he knew how clever she was, and he wanted her to reach her full potential by continuing her studies so that she would have a fantastic career and life in the future. She said he should have made her pregnant when they first met. But if he had, she would not be in the position she is today—she would not have gotten her second degree and gone on to her PhD studies, and she would not have the job she had now. He also mentioned that they had talked about buying a house and had even been to the bank to ask about a mortgage, but because he worked overseas, the bank would not give him one—but they were happy to give her one.

She seized on this and said, 'So you want me to be the breadwinner and provide you with a home? It should be the other way around. You are supposed to provide me with a home and family, and you have done neither.'

Harry found this to be really hurtful. He had always thought, perhaps stupidly, that they were a team working together to build a good future together, but it seemed not. Maybe it is a cultural thing. What was hers was hers, and what was Harry's was hers. She then went on to say that even if he had joined her in Shanghai, he would have felt out of his depth when she was with all her old friends from her university days in Tianjin. It made him wonder whether that episode with the old Chinese man in that Japanese restaurant years before, who had called her a prostitute, had anything to do with this decision; perhaps she just didn't want to be seen in public with him anymore, especially in China.

She was crying when he was saying goodbye, and she never answered when he told her that he still loved her and would always love her. They had always said that to each other at the end of their mails each day—that they would love each other forever. It was doubtful that he would ever see her again, but he still loved her with all his broken heart, even after all she had done to him. He would never forget her. She still haunted his dreams, and it would take him years to get over her—if he ever did. Why could it not go on forever? Why could it not go on forever?

As Harry looked back, once the dust had settled, maybe Lucy was right and he got it all horribly wrong. It could be his fault that things turned out as they did. They were very happy when they lived together in Beijing, in Leeds, in London, and in Pretoria; they shared happy times with lots of love, fun and laughter. It was only since they had been apart for over three years whilst she was studying for her PhD that things deteriorated, especially over the last few months. He was too busy thinking about her future instead of thinking about the now. Perhaps if they had not been apart and had bought a house and started a family when Lucy was younger, before she'd started her master's degree, things would have turned out differently and they would still be together. But having a family was not a reason for staying together if one was unhappy. He realised now that a family life for Lucy, given her lack of one when she was younger, was very important to her—more important than he'd ever imagined. He was not entirely sure, though, given her intelligence and her desire to achieve a good future for herself, that she would have been happy being a mother and housewife.

But all the what-ifs would not change things now. Sadly their relationship was beyond redemption, and he would have to accept this and get used to it, as hard as it was going to be—and it was very hard for him. He is still suffering now. All he knows is that he would always love her and would remember all of their happy times together. All that he has left now are happy memories. But past happiness is all very well, but it doesn't help him now when he needs it the most.